FIRE IN THE BLOOD

Pandia looked down at the book in her hand. Then as if he could not wait for her answer Lord Silvester asked: "Have you thought about me?"

"It would be . . . difficult to think of anything . . . else."

"That is what I hoped," he said. "Your face is always before my eyes, and even when you are not there I feel you beside me."

He paused, then he said: "Look at me! I want to see your eyes! I want them to tell me what you think."

The way he spoke made Pandia quiver, and once again the flicker of fire was there. She knew as they moved within her that she wanted him to kiss her, and she was afraid when he looked into her eyes that he would know exactly what she desired.

Very slowly she obeyed him because it was impossible to do anything else. As she raised her eyes to his she was spellbound.

She could see the fire blazing within him, and as something wild and wonderful leapt within her, she was drawn to him as if by a magical power that was irresistible. . . .

Bantam Books by Barbara Cartland
Ask your bookseller for the books you have missed

160 WISH FOR LOVE
161 MISSION TO MONTE CARLO
165 A MARRIAGE MADE IN HEAVEN
166 FROM HATE TO LOVE
167 LOVE ON THE WIND
169 A KING IN LOVE
170 JOURNEY TO A STAR
171 LOVE AND LUCIA
172 THE UNWANTED WEDDING
173 GYPSY MAGIC
174 HELP FROM THE HEART
175 A DUKE IN DANGER
176 TEMPTED TO LOVE
177 LIGHTS, LAUGHTER AND A LADY
178 RIDING TO THE MOON
179 THE UNBREAKABLE SPELL
180 DIONA AND A DALMATIAN
181 FIRE IN THE BLOOD

Fire
in the Blood

Barbara Cartland

BANTAM BOOKS
TORONTO · NEW YORK · LONDON · SYDNEY

FIRE IN THE BLOOD

A Bantam Book / January 1984

ISBN 0-553-23799-3

Published simultaneously in the United States and Canada

PRINTED IN THE UNITED STATES OF AMERICA

O   0 9 8 7 6 5 4 3 2 1

Author's Note

The Divine Selene, who was also called Mene by the Ancient Greeks, with her "golden crown illuminated the shadowy night!" Every evening when her brother Helios, the god of Sunlight, had finished his journey she "rose in the sky on her chariot drawn by shining steeds."

She loved Endymion, the King of Elis, whose tomb is still shown at Olympia and to whom Selene bore fifty daughters.

Endymion was hunting one day on Mount Latima, when he lay down to rest in a cool grotto where he fell asleep. Selene saw him and, captivated by his beauty, stole a kiss while he slept. Endymion asked Zeus to grant him immortality and eternal youth. Zeus consented on condition that he reposed eternally asleep.

Still Selene comes faithfully night after night silently to see her sleeping lover. It is thus that the rays of the amorous moon caress us sleeping mortals.

Selene was loved by Pan, who took the shape of a white ram and drew her into the depths of a wood in Arcadia.

Pandia, a daughter of Zeus and sister of Erse, the goddess of dew, was remarkable for her beauty among immortals.

Chapter One

1898

*P*andia put the holly wreath she had made on the grave, realising as she did so that the December frost had already killed all the flowers that had been placed there the previous day.

There had been only a few of them, mostly little bunches of paper roses or mistletoe from the people in the village, a wreath of white chrysanthemums from the Vicar, and one of yellow from the Doctor who had attended her father.

She could not help feeling it was not a very impressive tribute to a man who she believed had given inspiration and creative thought to those who were prepared to listen.

Then she told herself somewhat cynically that nobody these days seemed interested in a Greek Scholar or a man whose intellectual powers were far out of the ordinary.

She had loved her father and thought how handsome he looked, even when he was dead and she had seen him before he was lifted into his coffin.

She could understand how her mother had been brave enough to run away with him, incurring not only the wrath of her family but ostracism as far as they were concerned for the rest of her life.

Her mother and father had been very happy, which to Pandia was a consoling thought, and she believed fervently that they were together now and nothing would ever separate them again.

1

However, it was difficult for her to feel anything but lonely as she left the Churchyard to walk slowly back to the small Tudor house on the edge of the village where she had lived all her life.

It was not a large house, but when her mother had been alive it had been beautiful and filled with the love and happiness which Pandia felt now she would never find again.

It had been such fun, and she almost expected as she opened the front door to hear her father and mother laughing in the tiny room which he called his Study and in which he worked, and then to see her identical self come from the Sitting-Room.

Even to think of Selene, which she did as seldom as possible, made her feel unhappy.

Although she had half-hoped that her twin sister would come to their father's Funeral, she thought when it was over and there was no sign of her that it had really been a ridiculous idea.

Now Pandia took off the cloak she had worn over her shoulders, which, heavy though it was, had not prevented the biting December wind from making her shiver.

She went into the Study because, being the smallest room downstairs, it was the easiest to keep warm, and found as she expected that Nanny had lit the fire while she was out.

The flames were leaping above the logs, sending a glowing light over the worn leather armchair in which her father had always sat.

For a moment she almost imagined she could see him there.

Then she told herself that people who were bereaved always thought they were seeing visions or hearing voices and she must be sensible.

As soon as she was a little warmer she would settle down to copying out, in her neat and elegant handwriting, the last translations from the Greek that her father had done before he had been taken ill.

She was praying that the Publisher who had accepted two of his other manuscripts would like this one.

Even so, it would make very little money.

At the same time, she felt it would please her father to know there was another thin volume of his work ready for the public, if they were interested enough to buy it.

"I wonder why it is," Pandia asked herself, and it was a question she had asked many times before, "that Papa's work, which is so moving and inspiring, should remain unsold, while people buy the most terrible trash which would not inspire a frog!"

Then, because she knew the answer, she laughed.

"At least, Papa," she said aloud, "I loved everything you translated, and so did Mama, and perhaps one day you will be discovered as so many other great writers have been."

It was a fantasy she had often told herself in the past, imagining that suddenly, out of the blue, her father, like Lord Byron, would become famous overnight.

People would flock down to the village where they lived to tell him how much they admired him and perhaps to offer him an appointment at one of the Universities.

Then, because the fairy-story had to go on in her mind, Pandia imagined herself entertaining other Scholars of the same brilliance as her father, and perhaps a number of under-graduates would look up to him in admiration and become his pupils.

It was a story that was never to become reality because her father had remained unnoticed.

There was no enthusiasm for the books he wrote, and on the Publisher's part only an indifference which was somehow more hurtful than if he had said definitely he had no wish for any more volumes.

The amount of money they brought in was infinitesimal, and Pandia often thought they would really have starved if it had not been for the small income that came from a legacy to her mother.

This she had left to her twin daughters before she died.

In a way, Pandia thought, it was lucky that Selene did not want her share and had left home two days after her mother's death.

Even now, after three years of silence from her twin, Pandia could still feel bewildered that she should have gone away without saying good-bye and leaving only a note.

She could see the expression of consternation on her father's face as vividly as if it were etched on her memory.

She could still feel the kind of emptiness within herself she had felt when she read what Selene had written.

I have gone to find Mama's relations and ask if I can live with them. I cannot stand this boring little village any longer, and being so poor and miserable.

Please do not try to get in touch with me, as I have made my decision and will not alter it.

Selene.

That was all!

There had been no word of affection, no vestige of regret for her father, who had always loved her, or for her twin sister, who had thought they were indivisible.

In fact, Selene had never loved them, Pandia had realised bitterly.

She had thought that she and Selene were so close that they would be miserable without each other, and she had always believed that twins were different from other people.

Because they looked so identical that no one could tell them apart, it was hard for Pandia to face the truth and know that in every other way there was no resemblance between them.

Thinking back after Selene had gone, she supposed she had always known that her sister was ambitious socially and was bored by the quiet life they all lived because they could not afford anything else.

When they were alone Selene had often said:

"How could Mama have been so stupid as to run away from her home and give up the rich, comfortable life she had there?"

"She fell in love with Papa," Pandia had said.

"But he was only a Tutor to her brothers!"

"Papa comes from a noble family in Hungary," Pandia had argued. "They may not be rich, but their blood is blue, if that is what interests you."

"How could it interest me?" Selene had snapped. "It is no consolation to think that Mama threw away her rich blue blood for a very inferior brand of poor Hungarian!"

Pandia had been shocked.

"You should not talk like that, Selene! It is very disloyal to Papa, who is so clever. His translations from the Greek are brilliant!"

Selene had shrugged her shoulders.

"Who else thinks so except you, and of course, Mama?"

She spoke scathingly and Pandia knew uncomfortably that Selene looked at their mother disparagingly because in her eyes she had done something incredibly foolish which had unfortunately affected them all.

Often when her father was not present they would beg their mother to talk of the old days when she had lived in the large Georgian mansion in Oxfordshire.

Her father, who was Lord Gransden, had been of great importance not only in the County but also because he had a place at Court.

He was Master of his own fox-hounds, was Lord Lieutenant of Oxfordshire, and was a man, her mother told them with pride, whom everybody looked up to and respected.

Because of the way her mother described him, Pandia's grandfather became so real to her that she listened wide-eyed to the tales of the garden-parties, important dinners, and Hunt Balls that took place at his house.

Then there were the dances to which her mother was invited both in Oxfordshire and in London, and as soon as she became a débutante she had made her curtsey at Buckingham Palace.

It was all like a fairy-story to Pandia, and it was only afterwards that she realised that to Selene it would have been a Paradise which she resented she could never enter because her mother had deliberately left it and closed the door behind her.

"I want to go to Balls when I am old enough!" Selene had raged when they were alone in their bedroom after one of their mother's reminiscences. "I want to live in a huge house, have horses to ride, luncheon and dinner-parties every day, and of course I want expensive gowns!"

She walked across the room as she spoke to stare at herself in the mirror.

"I am beautiful! I know I am beautiful, but who sees me here? Only a lot of village idiots and giggling choir-boys!"

Pandia had no answer.

She was only afraid that Selene's outbursts would be overheard by her mother, who would be deeply hurt.

It must have been when her mother fell ill, and it was obvious that she was growing weaker and weaker, that Selene had made up her mind to leave home, and only waited until the Funeral was over to do so.

When she was alone in her room, Pandia wept bitterly.

"How could she do anything so cruel and unkind?" she asked herself, and hoped passionately that Selene would change her mind and come back again.

But there was no sign of her, and because she appeared not to need money, Pandia supposed she must have succeeded in persuading her mother's family to accept her, and was now living the way she wanted to do.

At that time Selene had been nearly sixteen, and now Pandia remembered that on their next birthday, which was in two months' time, she and Selene would be nineteen.

She had hesitated for a long time before she had written to her to say that their father was dead.

She had addressed the letter to her grandfather's house in Oxfordshire, hoping that if Selene was not there the letter would be forwarded on to her.

She wondered if she had changed very much from the rebellious young girl who had resented living in obscurity and longed for a different kind of life altogether.

"Perhaps she no longer looks like me," Pandia told herself.

She sat staring into the mirror, knowing without conceit that in the intervening years she had actually grown far more beautiful than she had been at sixteen.

The red lights in her hair, which came from her father's Hungarian blood, make a striking contrast to her pale, translucent skin.

Her eyes had always seemed enormous, and now that she had lost what her mother used to call the "puppy fat" of childhood, her face seemed almost too small for them.

She had a straight little nose and perfectly curved lips, which were never noticed because people looked first at her large eyes.

Fringed with dark lashes, they were, in some lights, a strange green and in others mysterious with the darkness of dusk.

They were very expressive eyes, mirroring her emotions, her feelings, and even her thoughts.

She was quite sure that Selene's would be the same.

In the past she had always known exactly what her twin was thinking, and when Selene was angry her eyes would seem to flash with a fire that smouldered in the very depths of them.

When she was happy her eyes were not only green but filled with sunshine.

"I hope she is happy now," Pandia told herself as she walked through the Hall towards the kitchen.

She could hear Nanny, who was getting old and rather slow, rattling the sauce-pans.

Although she did not feel at all hungry after the emotional strain of her father's Funeral, she knew she could not disappoint Nanny by refusing to eat anything she cooked.

"Is that you, Miss Pandia?" Nanny called out as she drew nearer to the kitchen.

"I am back," Pandia replied. "It is very cold outside!"

"I've made up the fire in the Study for you."

"I saw you had," Pandia answered, "and it was sweet of you to remember it. I thought perhaps I could give you a hand in the kitchen."

"I'm all right," Nanny said. "You go and get warm. I don't want you down with a chill."

There was a touch of panic in her voice, with which Pandia was familiar, and it was because, as she knew, Nanny had never stopped blaming herself for the cold which had caused her mother's death.

She felt that somehow she could have made the house warmer and insisted on her mother buying herself a thicker winter coat.

Because she thought it would please Nanny, Pandia said:

"All right, I will go back to the Study. Call me when you are ready."

Nanny did not answer, and she walked back the way she had come, thinking that they were very fortunate to have such a large supply of logs piled up outside the back door.

There were also at least three bags of coal in one of the out-houses, but coal was expensive and they used it sparingly.

At the same time, Pandia knew she had to think not only of herself but of Nanny, who was getting on for seventy.

She had lived with them ever since she and Selene were born, and, Pandia thought now, she was the only family she had left.

But Nanny, kind and understanding though she was, could not fill the gap that had been left by losing her father.

They had been so close these last years, especially since he had become ill and had talked to her as if she were his contemporary.

"You may look like a woman, my dearest," he had said to her once, "and a very beautiful one at that, but you have the intelligence and the brain of a man. If I had a son, which I would like to have had, he would have been no cleverer than you are."

"Thank you, Papa, that is a wonderful thing to say to me," Pandia had answered.

She had worked hard to please him, and while she and Selene had been taught by a Governess, who fortunately lived in the village, it was with their father that they studied all the major subjects.

They learnt Greek and other foreign languages as well as studying English literature and geography.

Geography for them was a very comprehensive subject, for their father believed that to understand the world they must do more than look at a country as a place on the map. They had to learn about the customs and nature of the people who lived in each land and were different from those of every other nation.

Pandia found it absorbing, though she knew without her putting it into words that it bored Selene.

"I want to meet people, not just learn about them," she had said to Pandia when they were alone. "What is the point of my hearing what wonderful riders the Hungarians are when the only horses I have a chance of riding are no more than hobblers fit only for the knacker's yard?"

"That is not true!" Pandia had expostulated. "Because Papa and Mama are so popular, the farmers are kind to us, and the horse I was riding two days ago was so spirited that I had the greatest difficulty in controlling him."

"I want the best horses," Selene had pouted, "and I want to hunt with a smart pack."

There was nothing like that in their village.

In fact, Bedfordshire was a flat, rather dull County, with very few large houses and with great stretches of agricultural land which had gained it the nickname of being the "Kitchen-Garden of England."

To Pandia it had a strange beauty of its own, and she loved the slow-moving river Ouse at the bottom of their garden and the meadows through which it wound its way.

There she would find mushrooms in the spring and a profusion of cowslips, and when the fields were white with snow, as they were now, the wild hares went coursing away as soon as she appeared.

But to Selene everything was flat and dull, and looking back Pandia was now not really surprised by the way she had gone without saying good-bye.

The Study seemed to welcome her with a warmth that enveloped her as soon as she opened the door.

She crouched down on the hearth-rug, saying as she did so:

"I wonder what I am to do now, Papa. Do you think I am clever enough to go on where you left off?"

She almost expected to hear her father reply in his deep voice, which, although he spoke perfect English, still had a faint trace of a Hungarian accent in it.

When there was only silence she gave a little sigh.

"I suppose for the first time in my life I shall have to make up my own mind." she said, "and that is going to be difficult because I have always relied on you."

She knew she would never have the strength, or was it the nerve, to do as Selene had done, but she supposed because they were twins they were the complement of each other.

"The other half," as Nanny often said.

Selene was determined and obstinate, forceful, and had a will of iron.

Pandia knew she was indecisive, gentle, frightened of

hurting people, and quite incapable of being ruthless or determined if there was any opposition.

"It is wrong to be like that, I am sure it is," she told herself, "but there is nothing I can do about it."

Then she thought she heard Nanny calling her, and putting the guard in front of the fire she walked towards the door.

As she reached it she instinctively looked back to see if her father was sitting comfortably in his armchair and had everything he wanted.

Then because the chair was empty she felt a pain in her heart that was physical and wondered how long it would be before she ceased to think of him almost every moment of the day.

She went back into the small Hall which she and her mother had painted a pale green because the dark panelling which had been there for ages made it seem small and shabby.

Then, when having closed the door behind her she would have gone into the kitchen, there came a loud rat-tat on the front door.

Pandia wondered who it was, knowing that anybody from the village would have called at the kitchen-door.

It took her only two steps to turn the handle and open it.

For a moment she stood as if turned to stone and thought she must be dreaming.

Standing in the porch was Selene.

She was so smart, so exquisitely dressed, enveloped with fur and with ostrich-feathers in her fashionable hat, that Pandia was astonished that she instantly recognised her! But Selene's face was still so like her own that she was unmistakable.

"Selene!"

Somehow the words seemed to be jerked from between her lips, and Selene, almost pushing past her, walked into the Hall.

"You are surprised to see me?" she asked.

"Yes, of course," Pandia answered. "But you are too late. Papa was buried yesterday."

"I know that," Selene replied, "but I have come to see you. Who else is in the house?"

With an effort Pandia shut the front door because the wind was blowing through it.

She was aware as she did so that a very smart carriage drawn by two horses, with a coachman and a footman on the box, was moving away.

"Only Nanny," she replied in answer to Selene's question. "Where is your carriage going?"

She had the frightening feeling that Selene had come home to stay, and was wondering if she would be comfortable enough and what they would give her to eat.

"I told them to rest the horses at the Inn," Selene replied. "I suppose it is still there?"

"The Anchor? Yes, of course."

Pandia thought with relief that they would not have to feed the two men, and she said hurriedly:

"Go into the Study where it is warm, and I will tell Nanny you are here. I think luncheon is almost ready."

"I could do with something to eat," Selene replied. "I had forgotten how far away we lived from London. It has taken me hours to get here!"

She spoke as if it were Pandia's fault, but she obviously did not expect a reply as she went into the Study and her sister ran to the kitchen.

"Nanny! Nanny!" she cried. "Selene is back! She has just arrived!"

Nanny looked at her as if she thought her ears were deceiving her. Then she answered:

"Well, if she's come for the Funeral she's too late!"

"That is what I told her. She is hungry, and we will have to eat in the Dining-Room."

As she spoke, Pandia saw the change of expression in Nanny's face.

Because there had been only the two of them after her father had become confined to his bedroom, they had eaten together in the kitchen, but she was quite certain that Selene would dislike that and perhaps make a fuss.

"I will lay the table," Pandia said quickly, "and if you will put everything on a tray I will fetch it."

Nanny's lips tightened, but she did not say anything, and without waiting Pandia hurried into the Dining-Room, which was just beside the kitchen.

It was only a small room but her mother had made it very attractive.

The curtains were not of a rich material, but before they faded they had been a very pretty shade of ruby red, and they matched the seats on the chairs.

It all gave an impression of rich colour, and when her mother was alive there had always been a bowl of flowers in the centre of the table.

Pandia quickly found a clean white table-cloth and spread it over the table, then laid on it the knives, forks, spoons, and glasses.

A silver bowl which her mother had treasured was on the sideboard and she placed it in the centre.

Although there were no flowers at this time of the year, she thought the table looked very much the same as when they had all been there for meals.

Pandia laid it for only two people, knowing that Selene would not expect to sit down with Nanny.

Peeping into the kitchen, she saw that Nanny was dishing up the rabbit, which was giving out a delicious fragrance, and she hurried across the Hall to the Study.

"Luncheon will be ready in two minutes!" she said. "Would you like to wash, Selene, and take off your hat?"

"I suppose I might as well make myself comfortable," Selene answered.

She was sitting, Pandia noticed, in their father's chair, holding out her hands to the fire.

Now she was discarding her hat, and, looking at her without it on, Pandia thought she still looked exceedingly beautiful, but they no longer so closely resembled each other.

Then she realised that it was not Selene's face that had changed but the way she arranged her hair.

Also her eye-lashes seemed darker than they had been in the past, and her lips were redder.

While she was looking at her sister, Selene was looking at her.

"We are still alike," she said.

To Pandia's delight, she seemed pleased.

"I thought for a moment that you had changed," Pandia said, "but it is only the way you are doing your hair, and of course you look very beautiful."

"I thought you would admire me," Selene replied, "but in my position I am expected to be smart and of course expensively dressed."

"Your position?" Pandia enquired, puzzled.

"I am married," Selene answered. "Did you not know?"

"No, of course not! How should I?"

Selene laughed.

"I forgot that Papa was never interested in the newspapers, and I suppose in this dead-and-alive hole you would not be aware if the world came to an end!"

"I should have wanted to know that you were married," Pandia replied. "You might have written to tell me!"

Selene did not answer. She was busy patting her hair into place.

Then she rose to her feet, revealing as she did so her gown of rich peacock-blue silk, which had been concealed by the fur-trimmed coat she wore when she arrived.

Her waist was tiny and the bodice above it was moulded over her breasts in a way which made her look exceedingly elegant and also, Pandia thought, somewhat revealing.

Selene walked towards the door.

"I suppose there is nothing to drink?" she asked.

"I think we have a bottle of claret left, which Papa used to enjoy."

"Well, you had better open that," Selene replied. "I certainly need something to sustain me after such a long journey."

"I wish you had told me you were coming," Pandia said. "We could have had everything ready for you. However, Nanny has cooked a rabbit for luncheon, and as you will remember, her rabbits are always delicious!"

Selene laughed.

"I am not likely to forget it! Looking back, I can remember nothing but rabbit, rabbit, and rabbit, because it was cheap!"

Pandia did not answer. She was almost in the Dining-Room, looking for the claret.

The Doctor had thought a red wine might do her father good and he should have a glass at luncheon and another at dinner.

Pandia found that there was a little left in one bottle, and there was fortunately another one that was unopened.

She poured what was left into Selene's glass, and she sipped it with an expression of one who was about to take poison. Then she said:

"This is not as bad as I feared. Papa always had fairly good taste in wines."

"How would you know that?" Pandia asked.

She was thinking that Selene had been only nearly sixteen when she had left home.

"Oh, I used to take a sip now and then from the bottles in the Dining-Room just to see what the wine was like, and I thought then that being a foreigner Papa would prefer a good wine rather than the spirits which so many Englishmen drink."

"It sounds strange to hear you say 'foreigner' like that," Pandia remarked. "I never really thought of Papa being one."

"Of course he was a foreigner," Selene said, "a Hungarian teacher. And why Mama was so mad as to run away with him I cannot imagine."

Pandia had heard this before, and she was not surprised when Selene continued:

"If you could only see the house in which our grandfather lived. It is large and magnificent, and my house is not unlike it, but even larger!"

"Perhaps you would tell me your name, and to whom you are married," Pandia said in a small voice.

"My husband is the Earl of Linbourne," Selene replied.

There was no doubt of the note of satisfaction in her voice, and as if she could not help boasting she added:

"I am a Countess, and I enjoy every moment of it! Think of it, Pandia! I have the position in life I always wanted and longed for, the gowns I used to dream about, carriages to ride in, Thoroughbred horses to ride, and I attend so many Balls that I declare I am growing tired of them!"

She spoke like a small child who wishes to score off another, and Pandia said quietly:

"I am so glad for you, Selene. I remember Papa saying if we wanted something badly enough and willed it to happen, it would!"

"If Papa thought that, he might have willed us a little more money!" Selene replied sharply. "And Mama might not have died if she had not been so cold in this draughty house and grew weak because we could not afford good food."

Pandia gave a cry.

"Selene, that is not true! It is true you could not have all you wanted, but we always had enough to eat, and although we had to be very careful, we had practically everything we wished for."

"You may have done," Selene said scathingly, "but I hated the pinching and saving and having to make do with everything that was second- or even third-rate!"

Because she could not bear to hear her home disparaged in such a way, Pandia said quickly:

"Now you have everything you want."

"Everything!" Selene agreed.

"How long have you been married?"

"Over a year. I was married when I was seventeen

and eight months old. The Earl fell in love with me the moment he saw me."

"What is he like?" Pandia asked. "Tall and handsome?"

There was a little pause before Selene replied:

"He is older than I am, and of course I admire and respect him, and although he has been married before he has no heir to the title."

"Are you going to have a baby?" Pandia asked.

Selene shook her head.

"Not yet, thank goodness. I want to enjoy myself first. It is what I feel I am entitled to after living in this hovel for so long."

Pandia drew in her breath, but she let the remark pass and asked:

"Do tell me how our grandparents behaved after you arrived there. I have been curious for so long!"

"They were very kind," Selene said. "I told them Mama was dead and I had nobody to look after me, and they treated me as if I were their younger daughter. My uncles, the oldest of whom now is Lord Gransden, are charming too, although their wives are a little sour because I am so beautiful."

"I can understand their being jealous."

"Of course they are," Selene replied. "They grew more jealous as I grew older and were, of course, delighted when I got married, except that it made them angry to think of the spectacular social position I now hold."

It was obvious that Selene was boasting again, and Pandia, eating the rabbit which as usual Nanny had cooked to perfection, had the strange feeling that her sister was doing so for some ulterior motive she had not yet revealed.

She had always known what her twin was thinking, and now she had the feeling that Selene was acting a part and manoeuvring everything for her own ends, as she always had.

Selene finished the claret that was left in the bottle and surprised Pandia by asking her to open the other.

"I never imagined you would drink a lot of wine," she said as she looked for the corkscrew. "Mama never drank anything in the way of alcohol."

"That was because she was economising," Selene said. "I enjoy wine, especially champagne, if I am sharing it with somebody attractive."

"Did you have many offers of marriage before you accepted your husband?" Pandia enquired.

"I had three," Selene answered, "but they were of no importance. Actually I was married in my very first Season, and all the other débutantes who came out at the same time were wild with envy!"

"It must have been very exciting for you, but I wish, Selene, you had asked me to your wedding."

"I could not do that," Selene replied after a little pause.

"Why not? Are you ashamed of me?" Pandia asked.

She knew her twin hesitated and was wondering whether or not to tell the truth.

Then she said:

"I told our grandparents when I first went to them that both you and Papa, as well as Mama, were dead!"

Pandia gave a little gasp.

"You said that? Why?"

"Because I wanted to make certain they would look after me," Selene explained. "When I arrived saying I was all alone in the world, they could hardly turn me away from the door!"

For a moment Pandia could not speak. Then she said:

"I think it was wrong of you, if not wicked, to tell such terrible lies. It would have hurt Papa very much if he had known about it."

"There was no likelihood of his hearing about it," Selene replied. "Knowing where I was, he would not come looking for me, and if they thought he was dead, you had to be dead too."

"I cannot imagine why you wanted to tell them that."

Then as Pandia spoke she knew the reason just as clearly as if Selene had put it into words.

Her sister had always wanted to be the only one. She had never wanted a sister, least of all a twin.

"It is not natural," she had raged once, "that I should have to share everything with you, and that people look at us as if we were one person instead of two. I am mè, and I do not want to be half of you, or for you to be half of me!"

She had said it in a temper, and Pandia had forgotten it afterwards, but she knew now that it was what Selene had thought all the time.

When she had had the chance to be on her own she had taken it.

But there was nothing Pandia could do about it now, and there was no point in making a fuss.

Instead she poured the claret from the new bottle into Selene's glass and said:

"I hope you will enjoy this. It will certainly warm you up after your long drive."

Selene sipped a little of the claret and said condescendingly:

"Quite good!"

"And now, Selene," Pandia said, "tell me exactly why you have come."

There was a pause and for a moment she thought that Selene was not going to reply or, if she did, would not tell her the truth.

Then she said a little hesitatingly:

"I want—your help, Pandia—in a way that only you can—help me!"

Chapter Two

For a moment there was silence and Pandia looked astonished.

It seemed to her incredible that after Selene had been away for so long and never communicated with her in any way, she should now ask for her help.

Then, because she felt rather touched that her sister still found her useful, she replied:

"Of course I will help you if I can, Selene, but I cannot imagine how."

Selene took another sip of the claret as if she felt it would help her. Then she said:

"It is a rather strange story, but I had arranged a long time ago to be with somebody who matters to me for the next few days."

Pandia was listening intently but for the moment she could not imagine what Selene was going to say.

"I was, in fact," her sister went on, "leaving tonight to stay with this person. My husband had arranged to go on an important mission for the Government, but last week a relative of his unexpectedly died."

"I suppose your husband does not know about me?" Pandia said in a low voice.

"Of course not!" Selene said quickly. "He believes, as our grandparents did, that Mama, Papa, and you are all dead."

Her voice had sharpened as she spoke, and although Pandia told herself it was stupid to be hurt, she felt like

crying out despairingly at having been dismissed so
casually from her twin's life.

"As I was saying," Selene continued, "George left for
Paris early this morning, and I had planned to leave
London tomorrow morning, but now I am expected to
go to the Funeral."

"Whose Funeral is it?" Pandia asked, feeling she
should show some interest in what Selene was saying.

"It is the Duke of Dorringcourt who has died. He
was a very old man and I do not suppose many people
will mourn him, but George has said that I must represent him at the Funeral which takes place tomorrow."

There was silence, then Pandia said:

"I suppose. . .if the Duke was a relation. . .it would
be impossible for you to refuse."

"Quite impossible," Selene agreed. "But I cannot
waste my time in mourning the dead when I want to be
with somebody who is very much alive!"

The way she spoke made Pandia look at her in surprise,
and because she had always been able to read Selene's
thoughts she asked:

"Who is this person who means so much to you?
Your voice changes when you speak of. . .him."

Selene smiled.

"I suppose it will not matter my telling you," she
said, "but, Pandia, I am in love. . .wildly, crazily in
love!"

Pandia looked at her in astonishment.

"But. . .Selene. . .you are. . .married!"

"What has that got to do with it?"

"I should have thought that it was. . .if not impossible. . .very wrong to love. . .somebody else when
you are. . .married."

Selene gave a little laugh.

"I might have guessed that would be your attitude,
living in this hole, but I can assure you that in the
world outside, nearly everybody in my position, especially if they are as beautiful as I am, has a lover."

"Selene!"

Pandia was now very, very shocked.

"How can you say such things?" she asked. "Papa and Mama would be horrified!"

"Oh, do stop being so ridiculously old-fashioned, Pandia!" Selene snapped. "If that is the attitude you are going to take, I shall not tell you anything, and we never used to have any secrets from each other."

Pandia softened at once, and replied hesitatingly:

"Of course we had no. . .secrets in the. . .past, and I want you to. . .tell me everything. . .but it is. . .difficult for me to. . .understand the life you. . .lead now."

"Of course it is," Selene agreed, "being shut up here, seeing nothing of the world, and never meeting a decent-looking man from one year's end to another."

"Tell me about this. . .person whom you. . .love," Pandia said, wishing to divert Selene's criticism from herself.

Her sister put her arms on the table and rested her chin in her hands.

"He is wonderful, Pandia," she said, "the most wonderful, most attractive man I have ever met in my whole life!"

"And he loves you?"

"Of course he loves me in the same way that I love him! I never knew before that I could have such ec-static feelings!"

The way she spoke, with a note of passion in her voice that Pandia had never heard before, made Pandia feel very strange.

"But. . .Selene. . .what can you do about it. . .when you are married to the Earl?"

"It has been difficult to see Ivor as much as I have wanted to," Selene replied, "and when George said he was going to Paris, it was a Heaven-sent opportunity for us to be together."

"Where are you going?"

"I am not going to tell you or anybody else that," Selene replied, "but we shall be alone and for a few days at any rate I shall be in Heaven!"

Again there was that note of passion that sounded very strange, and as if she was aware of what Pandia was thinking, Selene said with a little laugh:

"At least Papa gave me something! I certainly have fire in my blood which I can tell you is very Hungarian!"

"It would upset Papa if it got. . .you into. . .trouble." Pandia said quickly.

"That is not likely to happen," Selene replied, "if I am careful and if you help me."

Pandia looked puzzled.

"How can I help you?"

"It is quite simple," Selene answered. "You must go to the Funeral of the Duke instead of me!"

Pandia stiffened and sat straight up in her chair.

"G-go to the. . .Funeral?" she faltered. "How can I. . .possibly do that?"

Selene bent forward towards her.

"It will be quite easy, Pandia," she said. "I will tell you exactly what you have to do, and while we have grown apart, we are still exactly alike."

"But nobody would. . .believe that I am. . .you!"

"In my clothes, driving in my carriage? Do not be so silly! Why should anyone question for one moment that you are not who you appear to be?"

"B-but. . .I would be. . .frightened! Supposing somebody. . .spoke to me and I did not know the. . .answers?"

Selene sat back in her chair.

"Really, Pandia! When I think how Papa used to rave about your brains and your intelligence and how much cleverer you were than I am, I can hardly believe you cannot do me this simple little favour."

"It does not sound. . .simple to me!" Pandia protested.

"There will be no difficulties, and after you have helped me as I know you will, because I do desperately need your help, you can come back here and disappear! Nobody will ever hear of you again or have the slightest idea that I have a twin sister who is still alive."

The way Selene spoke made Pandia feel that she

was very easily disposed of and of no consequence whatsoever.

At the same time, she thought that what Selene was asking her to do was frightening and extremely irresponsible.

She was quite certain that her mother would have thought it was something she should not do.

But how could she refuse Selene, who was, after all, the only relation she knew and who in the past had meant so much to her?

"Surely, Selene," she said aloud, "you could give up one day of being with this. . .gentleman who means so much to. . .you to go to the Funeral, and join him afterwards?"

"How can I do that?" Selene asked. "George will be returning on Friday, and every minute, every second Ivor and I are together is a joy and a rapture that we may never have the chance of again."

Because she thought Pandia was going to refuse her, she put out her hand, saying:

"Please, dearest, you used to love me, and I cannot believe that you of all people have changed over the years! Help me to be happy, Pandia, for just a few days."

She did not wait for her sister to reply but went on:

"It is not much to ask, and Ivor has been looking forward to it for so long that I cannot disappoint him."

The pleading note in her voice and her outstretched hand made it impossible for Pandia not to put her hand into her sister's and say:

"I will try. . .but if I fail you I know how. . .angry you will be."

"You will not fail, dearest," Selene said, "and thank you, thank you for being my friend and loving me enough to help me when I need it most."

Pandia felt her press her fingers, then she released them, saying:

"We must leave for London at once."

"I am to come with you. . .now?"

"Of course, and when we reach Linbourne House we have a great deal to do."

Pandia rose from the table. She felt as if her head were stuffed with cotton-wool, and she knew she was not thinking clearly.

One part of her mind was asking how she could do anything so strange and frightening, and yet her heart wanted to help Selene because she was her sister and her twin.

Selene rose too, and as she did so she said:

"You have always been so proud of your Hungarian ancestry, and at least the Hungarians are adventurous! From all I can remember Papa telling us about them, they never refused a challenge."

"That is true," Pandia answered, "and Papa was very dashing when he was a young man."

"Then tell yourself you are being like him," Selene said.

As she spoke she walked out of the Dining-Room, and Pandia had the idea that it was almost a triumphal march because she had got her own way, having worked on Pandia's feelings so cleverly that it had been impossible for her to refuse what her sister wanted.

When they reached the small Hall, Pandia said:

"Do you really mean me to come with you now?"

"Of course!" Selene said. "Because I am extremely efficient, I brought with me a perfect disguise so that none of the servants will see you until we have changed places."

Pandia did not know what she meant, but she went upstairs, took her best cloak from her wardrobe, and laid it on the bed as Selene came into the room.

She was carrying something in her hand, but before asking her what it was Pandia said:

"I am afraid I have only one black gown which I bought for Papa's Funeral, which is the one I have on."

"It looks cheap," Selene said, "but actually it is just what I want you to wear because this is what will be on your head."

She opened a small hat-box which she was carrying in her hand, and Pandia guessed she had collected it from her carriage, which had returned from The Anchor and was now waiting outside.

Selene drew from the box a bonnet which had a long black veil trailing from it.

For a moment Pandia looked at it in surprise, then she realised it was a widow's bonnet, and the crêpe veil which would cover her face was, as Selene said, a perfect disguise.

"I told the coachmen to wait outside so that he would not talk to Nanny and find out anything about you," her sister explained. "Now put on the bonnet and we will go downstairs, but be careful to keep your veil over your face so that the footman does not see you, and the same applies when we reach Linbourne House."

"What shall I take with me?" Pandia asked.

"Nothing," Selene answered. "All the things you will wear in London will be mine, and my maid will look after you and see that you have everything you need."

"Your maid?" Pandia asked. "She knows we are changing places?"

"Yes, of course," Selene answered, "and she is the only person I trust."

She gave a little laugh as she added:

"Yvette is French, and the French always have a *complice d'amour* in their love-affairs, so she knows exactly what is expected of her."

"'An accomplice of love,'" Pandia translated. "I remember seeing it written on some of the French prints which Papa had in a book."

"That is what Yvette is," Selene said, "and remember, she will be the only person who is aware that you are not me, and she will help you if there are any difficulties."

She saw the expression on Pandia's face and added firmly:

"There will be none, but hurry! You are wasting time and I want to be back in London as soon as possible."

"You are going to *him* tonight?" Pandia asked.

"Of course I am!" Selene replied. "George left this morning for Paris, and I am certainly not going to waste one moment of being with Ivor."

Pandia sat down at the dressing-table, put the widow's bonnet on her head, and pulled the veil down over her face.

The crêpe was so thick that it completely obscured her features and any glimpse of the red lights in her hair.

Selene was right. It was a very effective disguise.

Then as she rose to her feet, Selene put her thick cape over her shoulders while she was searching in a drawer for the black gloves she had worn yesterday for her father's Funeral.

"Now we will go downstairs," Selene said. "The carriage is waiting, and I think it would be a convincing remark if you say when you see it:

" 'What an elegant carriage! It is so kind of you to take me to London with you, and I shall be far more comfortable than if I were travelling on my own!' "

"I will say that," Pandia agreed.

She gave a little chuckle as she added:

"You are stage-managing everything, just as you did when we were children. It was always you who thought up the best charades!"

"I rather pride myself on my organising ability," Selene said, "but come on!"

"I must go and tell Nanny where I am going."

"Just tell her you are coming to London with me for two days, and you have no time to answer a lot of questions. You know what a 'Noscy Parker' she is!"

"That is unkind!" Pandia said quickly. "She has been wonderful in looking after us and doing everything because we could not afford any other servants."

Selene did not reply because she was already walking ahead of her down the stairs.

When Pandia caught up with her, she said:

"You must see Nanny before you leave. She would be broken-hearted if you left without talking to her."

"Of course I am going to see her," Selene replied, "and I will make all the explanations about your coming with me. I can do it much better than you can."

As she reached the Hall she looked at her sister and said:

"Throw back your veil. You do not want Nanny to think you look like a widow."

"No, of course not!" Pandia said humbly, thinking she should have thought of that herself.

They went into the kitchen, and as Nanny put down the plate she was drying she exclaimed:

"Miss Selene! Well, you're a stranger if ever there was one!"

"I know, Nanny," Selene said, "but you must not scold me! Just say: 'Better late than never!' as you used to do."

"You haven't changed much," Nanny said, looking her over, "despite all your frills and furbelows. You're just as you were, an' I expects just as discontented!"

"Now, Nanny, you are not to be unkind to me," Selene replied. "I am taking Pandia to London with me for two days because I think it would be good for her to have a change after being upset by Papa's Funeral."

"You should have been here yesterday," Nanny scolded, "and mournin' him respectfully."

"I know," Selene said humbly, "but it was impossible for me to get away, and as Pandia has forgiven me, you must too."

Nanny looked at Pandia for the first time since they had come into the kitchen.

"What's that you've got on your head, Miss Pandia?" she asked. "It's different from the bonnet you wore yesterday."

"I thought it would be warmer for her while we are driving to London," Selene said before Pandia could reply, "and with a foot-warmer for her feet and a fur rug over her knees, she will not catch cold in the carriage."

"That's right," Nanny said. "You look after your sister

for a change! It's been a long time since you left, and
not a word from you, nor even for that matter a present
at Christmas."

"I know, and it was very remiss of me," Selene
replied, "but now Pandia is coming with me to London,
and I will make up for it."

"While you're at it," Nanny said in her most authori-
tative tone, "your sister could do with some new clothes.
It's not right for her to wear the same threadbare gar-
ments year in an' year out, while from the look of it
you've got all the comforts!"

"You are quite right, Nanny," Selene agreed, "and I
will see that Pandia has lots of lovely gowns to come
home with."

"Now don't you forget," Nanny said, "as you've forgotten us these last three years!"

Selene looked at the kitchen clock and exclaimed:

"Quick, Pandia, we must hurry! It is a long way to
London, and we want to be there before it gets very
dark."

"Yes. . .of course," Pandia agreed.

She stepped forward and kissed Nanny on the cheek.

"Take care of yourself, Nanny," she said, "and I will
be back almost before you know I have gone!"

Selene did not kiss Nanny, but having reached the
door she said, waving her hand:

"Good-bye, Nanny! It has been lovely to see you
again!"

The two girls hurried through the Hall, and as they
opened the front door the footman quickly helped them
into the carriage.

There was, as Selene had promised, a foot-warmer
for their feet and a fur rug made of sable over their
knees.

As the carriage drove off, Selene, lying back comfortably against the soft padding, remarked:

"I must say Nanny looks a great deal older! Rather
like a wizened old gnome! But as you saw, I have not
forgotten how to handle her!"

"I do not know what we would have done without Nanny when first Mama was so ill. . .then Papa."

There was a little sob in Pandia's voice because she could not bear to hear Selene disparaging Nanny when she had looked after them ever since they were babies.

She remembered now that when they were small Selene had always been Nanny's favourite.

"I find old people tiresome," Selene replied.

The way she spoke made Pandia ask instinctively:

"You said your husband is older than you. How old is he?"

For a moment she thought her sister was not going to answer. Then Selene replied:

"George is nearly sixty!"

"Sixty! Why did you marry him?"

"Do not be silly, Pandia! Very rich Earls as distinguished as George are not lying about the place, and if they are, some ambitious Mama snaps them up before they realise what is happening!"

"But he is so very much older than you!"

"I know that, and I thought it did not matter, until I met Ivor."

"Who is Ivor?"

"You are being too curious," Selene said. "I am not going to tell you his full name, just in case you ever said something which might be repeated to George and make him suspicious."

"Selene! How could you think that I would do such a thing!" Pandia exclaimed. "Besides, you have made it clear that after I have helped you I am to return home to the country and disappear. You know there is nobody here who can talk of anything except growing vegetables."

"That is true," Selene conceded, "but because where Ivor is concerned I am afraid of my own shadow, I shall just tell you that he is Russian, he is a Prince, and he is so overwhelmingly attractive that women follow him as if he were the 'Pied Piper'!"

Pandia gave a little laugh, and Selene smiled as she added:

"But he loves me. He tells me he has never loved any other woman in his life in the same way."

"What a pity you did not wait a little longer so that you could have married him!"

Selene turned her head to look at her sister. Then she answered:

"Oh, dear, I keep forgetting how unsophisticated you are. Ivor is married! Of course he is married! Russians are betrothed almost when they are in the cradle! Fortunately, his wife is in Russia while he is here."

Pandia could hardly believe what she had heard. Then she said humbly:

"I quite understand, Selene, why you think me unsophisticated. At the same time, I think Mama would have been. . .shocked at your having a. . .love-affair with a. . .married man, when you have a. . .husband!"

"If you think I would do anything so silly as to run away as Mama did, you are very much mistaken!" Selene said. "I have no intention of causing a scandal, for, as you well know, if a woman is divorced she is ostracised by everybody in the Social World and might as well be dead!"

Pandia drew in her breath.

"Knowing that, you are. . .prepared to take the. . . risk?"

"There is no risk if you help me," Selene said. "If you are seen at the Funeral tomorrow, nobody is going to think for a moment that I am anywhere else. That will give me tonight and tomorrow night and Thursday with Ivor, since George does not return until Friday."

"He must not see me," Pandia said. "As your husband he might be able to tell the difference between us."

"There is no difference between us," Selene said firmly. "Nobody has ever been able to tell us apart."

Pandia was silent for a moment. Then she said:

"I was talking once to Papa about twins, after we had

been learning about Castor and Pollux, those Greek twins who belonged to the gods."

"I found them all very boring," Selene remarked.

"I said to Papa," Pandia went on, ignoring the interruption, "that when twins are identical, like you and me, it would be possible for them to play all sorts of tricks on people simply because nobody could tell them apart."

"That is what I have just said," Selene said impatiently.

"Papa replied," Pandia continued, "that if a man was in love with one of them, he would never be deceived by the other."

"I do not believe it!"

"Do you really think," Pandia argued, "that if I went instead of you to meet your Prince he would be deceived?"

Selene thought for a moment. Then she said:

"I do not know the answer to that. I am certain George would not notice. . .but that is different!"

"Are you saying that he is not in love with you?" Pandia enquired.

"Not in the same way," Selene said. "Besides, we have been married for a long time and George is not as young as he was."

What she said was very revealing, and Pandia could not help wondering whether her sister was truthful in saying that her marriage had brought her everything she wanted.

Material things, perhaps, but not the love and ecstasy she was finding, if regrettably, with another man.

Then as they travelled on, Selene, as if she could not help herself, began to talk to Pandia as she had in the old days, and now it was all about Prince Ivor.

"The moment I saw him, Pandia," she said as the horses carried them towards London, "I felt my heart turn a hundred somersaults, and I knew that he was the man I had dreamt about long before I left home."

"And did he feel the same about you?"

"Yes, of course! He said that when he looked at me

moving towards him across the Ball-Room at Devonshire House, he thought I was enveloped with a celestial light and that I was not a human being but a goddess from Olympus!"

"Papa would have understood that," Pandia said.

"If Papa had taught us more about gods who looked like Ivor, I might have found my Greek lessons more enjoyable!" Selene said. "As it was, I found them an unending bore!"

Pandia wanted to protest, but she knew it would be useless.

While she had thrilled to the stories of the philosophy, the mysticism, and the beauty of the ancient Greeks, and for her they had been an inspiration which had become part of her thinking, she was aware that for Selene it had been different.

She had wanted to share her enjoyment with her sister and had once said to her father:

"How can we make Selene realise how exciting what you are saying is, and how the Greeks altered the thinking of the whole civilised world?"

"There is nothing either of us can do," her father had said quietly, "and, my dearest, we must never expect from people more than they are capable of giving."

Pandia had often thought of the way he had said that, and she knew it was true.

She had known as the years passed that there was no use expecting Selene to be anything but herself, and she could not force beauty upon anybody.

Whether it was a beauty she saw with her eyes, heard with her ears, or felt in her heart, she could not give it to Selene.

Yet, the beauty which she and her father had enjoyed Selene had now found in a different way, she thought, even though she was shocked that it should be an illicit affair.

"Because I love him," her sister was saying, "I want to be perfect so that he will think me so. I want to be so beautiful that he can see no other woman's face but mine, and so clever that he wants to talk only to me!"

"I am sure nobody could be as beautiful as you, dearest," Pandia said.

"I hope not!" Selene replied. "And do not dare look so beautiful tomorrow, Pandia, that people tell me later they had never seen me 'look better'!"

She gave a scornful little laugh.

"That is about as effusive a compliment as any Englishman is likely to pay me! If only you could hear the things Ivor says!"

She made a rapturous little sound as she went on:

"He calls me 'Heart of my Heart,' or likens me to a star that has fallen from the sky, which he will keep captive forever!"

She spoke with a passionate note in her voice that Pandia did not miss. Then in a different tone she said:

"I will not lose him! Nobody shall take him from me! If any woman did, I swear I would kill her!"

"Selene, how can you talk like that?" Pandia asked.

"Does it sound very dramatic?" Selene replied. "Again it is my Hungarian blood, and it is Mama's fault if I am over-passionate. She should have married a nice, staid Englishman, so that we would have been unemotional, prim and proper young women whom everybody would commend!"

"In which case, we might not have been twins, and would certainly not have been beautiful!" Pandia replied.

Selene smiled.

"Perhaps you are right, and after all I should be grateful to Papa for that, if for nothing else!"

She did not wait for Pandia's answer, but went on:

"I used to hate him because Mama had run away with him and therefore we had none of the things that I wanted which should have been ours if she had not preferred a Hungarian Tutor to a nobleman like Grandpapa."

"How could you feel like that about Papa, who was so charming, so handsome, and so clever?" Pandia asked.

"I have often thought I shall never find a man like him, in which case I shall never marry!"

"You will be very stupid if you do not take the first opportunity you get!" Selene snapped. "After all, you cannot go on living alone with only Nanny to talk to for the rest of your life."

"I expect that is what I shall have to do," Pandia replied.

There was silence for a moment. Then she said:

"Sometimes I tell myself stories that because you miss me so much you invite me to stay with you, and introduce me to your friends."

She spoke dreamily, expressing in words what she had thought of so often, and was hardly aware that she was speaking aloud.

Selene gave a shrill scream.

"Of course that will never happen! Never! Never! I have told you that as far as our relations are concerned and all the friends I have made since I was married, you do not exist! You are dead, Pandia, from the point of view of the Social World, and you must never forget it!"

She paused before she went on:

"There must be a farmer or somebody in the village with whom you could settle down. The farms, if I remember, are quite comfortable, and I daresay you would be content. You never wanted the things I wanted."

Because Pandia knew her sister was deliberately disparaging her and speaking with a contempt that was very obvious in her voice, she felt she wanted to return home immediately.

Then she realised that she had already committed herself, having been stupid enough to let Selene manipulate her for her own ends and for her own selfish needs.

Selene had no love for her and never had, and the only reason she had been nice since she had suddenly reappeared was to make use of her.

She had made herself pleasant to Nanny while really despising the old woman who had nursed her, loved her, and made her childhood a very happy one.

"Why did I ever agree to this ridiculous farce?" Pandia silently asked herself.

She knew it was because, whatever Selene might feel about her, she still loved her twin.

There was a link between them which no amount of unkindness or even cruelty could break.

They had been born at the same time on the same day and under the same stars, and whatever happened, even if they never saw each other again, they were still in some strange manner indivisible.

She was silent for so long that Selene looked at her sideways, as if she thought she had been too unkind, or perhaps actually the word was too "frank."

"It is no use thinking of the future, Pandia," she said. "Let us just think that we are together now, and it is just like the old days."

Pandia knew that again Selene was placating her, and because she could not bear a scene she was ready to be placated.

"You will never know how much I have wanted to see you again and talk to you," she said quietly, "and now that we are together, go on telling me about yourself so that I can think about it after it is all. . .over."

Selene was only too willing, and she told Pandia how rich her husband was and how generous in giving her jewellery, gowns, and anything else she wanted in the various houses that he owned.

"Of course," she said, "he is set in his ways. I suppose every man becomes that with age. He is desperate to have a son, and if I gave him one I think he would cover me with diamonds from head to foot!"

Her voice expressed her excitement at the idea, and she went on:

"He has also promised to settle a large sum of money on me so that when he dies I shall be a very rich widow!"

"Then why are you not having a baby?"

Pandia knew as she spoke that it was a question which Selene did not want to answer.

Then, as if it was somehow a relief to be able to talk about it, she replied:

"I do not know, Pandia, and that is the truth. I am sure I ought to have had one by now, but I am afraid, desperately afraid, that George is too old."

"Papa always said," Pandia replied hesitatingly, "that. . .identical twins often do not have. . .children of their own."

"I have heard that too," Selene said, "and without telling George I went to see a Physician. He is Queen Victoria's Doctor, as a matter of fact."

"What did he say?"

"He said it was a lot of nonsense and he could show me dozens of identical twins who had had babies of their own."

Selene's voice dropped until it was little more than a whisper as she added:

"You must never tell anybody, because it sounds very immodest, but he examined me and said there was nothing wrong with me at all! He was actually quite certain I could have dozens of children without any trouble."

"I am glad, so very glad!" Pandia cried.

Then a thought struck her and she looked hastily at her sister.

"You. . .you do not think. . .Selene. . .that when you are. . .with the Prince. . .?"

There was no need to say any more.

Selene's chin went up and she answered:

"Why not? I know that if I have a baby, George would welcome it with such joy that it would never occur to him for one moment that it was not his!"

Pandia drew in her breath.

It seemed to her that suddenly the world was very different from what she had thought it was.

Never in her wildest imaginings could she have believed that in her own life there would be people like Selene behaving in the same strange and immoral man-

ner that she had believed could be found only in the
stories of the gods.

When studying Greek mythology with her father she
had been intrigued by the stories of how goddesses had
been attracted to handsome men with whom they were
unfaithful to their celestial husbands.

The gods on their part assumed the guises not only of
mortal men but of animals and pursued exquisite nymphs.

The tales had never seemed real, only fairy-stories to
explain the natural elements, like the sun, the moon,
the stars, and yet here in real life Selene was behaving
as her namesake had done.

Because her twin had always seemed to her so
beautiful, Pandia had been able to think of her in the
words her father had translated for her from the original
Greek, in which she was the moon:

After bathing her lovely body in the ocean she
clad herself in splendid robes and rose in the sky
in her chariot drawn by shining steeds. . .

Pandia could imagine Selene doing this all too clearly,
and she would look up in the sky to see her golden
crown which illuminated the shadowy night.

Now she remembered that her father had told her
how Selene had attracted Zeus, who had made her the
mother of three daughters, but that she loved to distrac-
tion Endymion, the handsome King of Elis.

Then she told herself that she did not want to think
about it.

The story of the goddess had ended in tragedy, and
she wanted Selene to be happy.

"Will she ever be able to find happiness if what she is
doing is wrong?" she wondered as the carriage drove on
towards London.

But with Selene still talking rapturously of Prince
Ivor, she could find no answer to her question.

Chapter Three

Linbourne House in Grosvenor Square was very impressive, and Pandia longed as they walked into the marble Hall to look round and see some of the main rooms.

But Selene hurried her up the staircase and into her bedroom, which overlooked the back of the house.

It was very magnificent, as she might have expected, tall and square with a huge bed draped with silk curtains from a carved corona.

As soon as they entered the room, Selene pulled the bell, saying as she did so:

"Now you can throw back your veil, but be careful that nobody sees you except Yvette."

"This is a very large house!" Pandia said. "I suppose the Reception-Rooms are very lovely."

"I can give parties for a hundred people without there being a crowd!" Selene said in her boastful voice. "But you must come and look at my *Boudoir*."

She opened another door and Pandia saw a room which was exactly what she had always imagined a *Boudoir* would be like.

The curtains were softly draped, the sofa and chairs were piled with silk cushions, and there were little tables with *objets d'art* on them and a profusion of hot-house flowers.

It seemed incredible in the middle of winter that

there should be huge carnations and purple, white, and green orchids.

Pandia could not help thinking of how much they must have cost, while her father and mother had had to count every penny.

Then she told herself that there was no use, as her father had said, expecting people to give more than they were capable of giving.

That certainly applied to Selene, but it still seemed incredible that she should so easily have disposed of their father and herself and doubtless never given either of them a thought until now.

'I hope Papa never knows how little she cared for him,' she thought.

Because she was so certain that he was still with her, she was afraid that he would know, and yet perhaps he would understand.

"Do you see that picture on the wall?" Selene was saying. "George bought it for me on one of his previous visits to France. It is a Boucher and it cost him thousands of pounds."

"It is beautiful!" Pandia exclaimed enthusiastically. "I have always wanted to see one!"

There was a door on the other side of the *Boudoir*, and Selene said:

"George's room is through there. He redecorated this whole Suite as soon as I married him, and allowed me to choose the curtains, the carpets, and of course the chandeliers, which came from Venice."

"It is all a perfect background for you," Pandia said.

Because she was pleased at the compliment, Selene smiled at her as she used to do in the old days without being affected.

Then there was the sound of somebody in the bedroom, and Selene said:

"That is Yvette. Come along, we must get busy."

Yvette was a Frenchwoman with sharp, shrewd eyes, and as they moved back into the bedroom, she stared at them in astonishment.

Then she clasped her hands together and said in French:

"*C'est extraordinaire!* I not believe two ladies look *justement* the same!"

"You do see, Yvette," Selene said, "that nobody will suspect for a moment that I am not attending the Funeral tomorrow."

"*Oui, c'est impossible, Madame!*"

"Then let us get on," Selene said. "Where is my gown? I suppose I shall have to wear the cloak in which my sister arrived."

"*Mais oui, Madame,*" Yvette agreed. "I pack two trunks, M'Lady, and send downstairs, you give the lady old clothes for charity *pour pauvres maîtresses.*"

Selene laughed and said to Pandia:

"Poor Governesses! Yvette is so clever! As you see, I could not manage without her."

"I suggest, *Mademoiselle,*" Yvette said, "you undress and go bed. I say downstairs want dinner up here, after long journey *très fatiguée.*"

"I shall want your widow's bonnet," Selene said, "and perhaps it is prophetic I should wear one!"

Pandia was shocked that she should be hoping that her husband might die, but she knew it was no use saying so.

She merely lifted the widow's bonnet with its long crêpe veil from her head and put it down on a chair.

Selene took off the very elegant blue gown in which she had travelled, and after she had washed, Yvette helped her into a black one which was very unlike the one which Pandia was wearing.

She saw to her surprise that it was an evening-gown with the bodice cut extremely low, with ruched tulle over her bare shoulders which matched the rows of tucks on the hem of the skirt.

Because she had the same white skin and red lights in her hair, Pandia, watching, felt almost as if she were seeing herself.

She realised for the first time how sensational both of

them could look in black, and when Yvette had hooked up Selene's gown at the back, her waist was so tiny that Pandia was sure it could easily be spanned by a man's two hands.

"You look wonderful!" she exclaimed.

"George does not like me in black," Selene replied. "I think really he is jealous because I look too spectacular, but Ivor will adore it!"

Pandia felt a little embarrassed because she was speaking so intimately in front of her maid, but it was obviously an ordinary occurrence, because Selene went on:

"Ivor adores me whatever I wear or do not wear. He says there is nobody in his eyes as beautiful as I am."

"If *Monsieur le Prince* saw you both," Yvette joined in, "he think he drink too much wine!"

"He is not going to see my sister," Selene said firmly, "and do hurry, Yvette! I want to leave!"

There was a necklace of emeralds for Selene to wear round her throat, and she also clasped an emerald bracelet round her wrist.

"I put ear-rings in hand-bag, *Madame*, with ring," Yvette said. "You put on when you arrive."

"Yes, of course," Selene agreed. "Did you order a carriage?"

"*Oui, Madame,* I ordered closed Brougham. Also say how kind of M'Lady send poor friend home with trunks so not have to hire Hackney-Carriage."

"You think of everything," Selene approved. "Now give me the widow's bonnet."

She put it on her head very carefully so as not to crush her hair, then Yvette covered her shoulders with a long black chiffon scarf before she put Pandia's heavy dark cloak over the top of it.

Selene made a face.

"What a shabby old cloak!" she exclaimed. "Have you nothing better than this to wear?"

"It is my best," Pandia replied, "but I have had it for some time because I bought it when Mama died."

"You had better find *Mademoiselle* one of those cloaks

I told you to throw away," Selene said. "They are certainly better than this!"

"I find, *Madame*," Yvette replied.

As she spoke she put the emerald ear-rings into an elegant satin hand-bag and handed it to Selene, saying as she did so:

"Hide, *Madame*, but stupid footmen notice nothing!"

"One never knows," Selene answered, "and we must take no chances!"

"*Non, non, Madame*."

Selene kissed Pandia perfunctorily and said:

"Now do not forget—you drive from here to the Funeral. When it is over they will expect you to go back to the Castle for something to eat, then you return quickly."

"You. . .you did not say I had to. . .go to the Castle!" Pandia exclaimed.

"Of course you will have to! You must realise that the relatives will be expected to meet and commiserate with one another!"

"But. . .I shall not. . .know them!"

"Neither do I!" Selene answered. "You do not think I waste my time with a lot of old people who should have been in their graves long ago? The Duke was ninety!"

Pandia wanted to say that he was still a relative, but Selene went on:

"You do not have to say much. Just smile, look gracious, and leave as soon as possible. Yvette will be waiting for you here, and on Thursday it might be a good idea to say you are tired and stay in bed."

Pandia wanted to expostulate that that would be very dull when she had never been to London before, but she was aware that Selene would not listen to anything she had to say.

Her sister pulled the black veil over her face, then as Yvette opened the door she turned back to say audibly:

"Good-bye, My Lady, and I can never thank you enough for all your kindness. You have been so generous!"

Then she was gone, and Yvette stood watching her

until she reached the top of the stairs, then came back into the bedroom and shut the door.

"Now, *M'mselle*," she said cheerfully, "*Je fait attention a vous.*"

She stared at Pandia and exclaimed again:

"*C'est extraordinaire!* I nevaire see twins look so alike! An' never two so very, very beautiful!"

"You are very kind," Pandia murmured, "but you do realise I am afraid of doing something wrong?"

"Not worry, *M'mselle. Milor'* away an' nobody in house—enjoy yourself!"

"I. . .I will try," Pandia said humbly.

Yvette helped her to undress. Then she found that Selene had her own private bathroom, which was on the other side of her bedroom.

"A bathroom!" Pandia exclaimed. "That is something new! Mama always told me that ladies bathed in their bedrooms and the water was carried upstairs in brass cans."

"*Madame* say idea from America," Yvette explained. "She see bath in house of Duke of Marlborough an' persuade *Milor'* she have same."

Pandia smiled.

She could imagine how Selene would have disliked anybody having something better than she had and would be determined not to be outdone.

It was certainly a very pretty bathroom. The walls were decorated in pink and hung with mirrors in which she was sure her sister admired herself.

It was delightful to soak in the warm scented water, and when she had dried herself with a soft towel embroidered with the Earl's monogram, Yvette brought her the most exquisite nightgown she had ever seen.

It was almost transparent and inset with lace.

When she got into the large comfortable bed and found that there was lace on the sheets and round the pillow-cases, Pandia felt as if she were a Princess in a fairy-tale.

The dinner that was sent up was so delicious that she found herself wishing she could share it with her father.

Being Hungarian, he appreciated good food, and her mother and Nanny had struggled to produce all sorts of different dishes to please him.

They experimented not only with rabbit and chicken, which were cheaper than meat, but also with vegetables which the farmers were usually only too pleased to give them from their surplus crops.

'Papa would have enjoyed this,' Pandia kept thinking as she ate a mousse which seemed to melt in her mouth, followed by pheasant cooked with wine, which was a game-bird she very rarely tasted.

There were several other unusual dishes before the meal was finished.

"I am sure if I ate like this every day," she said to Yvette, "I should grow very fat!"

The maid laughed.

"You're too thin, *M'mselle*, an' Her Ladyship's always afraid of adding even one *centimetre* round the waist. Then she eat nothin', and is *très désagréable*."

The way Yvette spoke made Pandia laugh, but she thought that with what they could afford at home, she was very unlikely to put on any weight.

After her dinner was finished Yvette brought her all the newspapers and magazines that she had noticed were laid out on a stool in the *Boudoir*.

She lay back against the pillows to look at the fashions in *The Ladies Journal* and the pictures of Society Beauties.

Not one of them was as lovely as Selene, but she found a photograph of her on one page and thought that tomorrow she would ask Yvette if she could take it home with her.

'Perhaps in the Court Circulars there have been references to Selene which I have missed,' Pandia thought.

Then she remembered that if there had, she would not have recognised her sister's name because she had not known she was married.

It still hurt her to think how her twin could have cut her so completely out of her life that she had not even written to tell her about that.

Then, because she was very tired after all the emotional strain of her father's Funeral yesterday and also from the conflicting feelings she had about Selene, she blew out the light and was ready to go to sleep.

Before she finally slipped away into a dream-world of her own, she could not help thinking of the Funeral tomorrow, and being apprehensive about the part she must play.

Supposing somebody realised she was not Selene? Supposing she was exposed?

Knowing what trouble it would cause and how furious Selene would be with her, she sent up a little prayer to her mother.

"Please, Mama, you know how to behave so much better than I do. Help me. . .help me to deceive everybody! Do not let anybody be. . .suspicious."

Then she found herself remembering Selene saying that it was a challenge which no Hungarian would refuse, and she could almost see her father's eyes twinkling.

"I only wish you were coming with me, Papa," she said to him. "You snapped your fingers at all the pomposity of the English aristocrats and persuaded Mama to run away with you. If you can do that, why should I worry about a simple Funeral?"

As she fell asleep she felt she could hear her father laughing.

*   *   *

Yvette woke Pandia early because she said she had to work on her hair.

It was quite a job, because it was far longer and thicker than Selene's, to arrange it in exactly the same way, but when Yvette had finished, Pandia agreed that it made her look exactly like her sister.

"I not finished, *M'mselle*," Yvette said. "When *Milor'*

absent, *Madame* use a little powder on her face and touch of dye on eye-lashes."

"Mama would have considered it very fast for a Society Lady to make up her face in such a way," Pandia said. "I know that actresses do so, but not ladies!"

"Many ladies do in secrecy in bedroom," Yvette said. "They cannot allow Gaiety Girls to be more attractive than they!"

Pandia laughed.

"I can understand that would be a disaster!"

She was speaking lightly, and Yvette said:

"Men are men, *M'mselle*, an' pretty face *irrésistible!*"

The way she spoke made Pandia wonder if Selene's husband had ever looked at anybody but her.

Then she told herself that as Selene was so lovely, it would be impossible for any Gaiety Girl to be her rival.

In a way, although it still shocked her, she could understand how the Prince and, from what Selene had said, a number of other gentlemen had been bowled over completely by her.

Yvette was touching the tips of her eye-lashes with a little brush, and it certainly made her eyes look even more fantastic than they did normally.

Then there was a touch of red salve for her lips and a dusting of powder which made her skin look whiter than ever.

She stared at herself in the mirror, realising that she actually looked as sensational as Selene had done before she left last night.

Although Selene had said she should wear her clothes, Pandia had not expected to be dressed in them from top to toe.

Never had she worn anything so delectable as the silk chemise that was trimmed with real lace and the black silk stockings that made her legs look so elegant she could not believe they were her own.

She put on a petticoat with row upon row of insertion that ended with a wide frill at the hem.

The black gown she now wore was very different from the black gown she had bought in Bedford.

Her arms and neck showed through the chiffon, and the gown had decorations of black velvet, which made it seem almost too frivolous and certainly too beautiful to be worn at a Funeral.

There was a necklace of pearls to wear round her neck and pearls for her ears.

"Is it correct to wear jewellery at a Funeral?" Pandia asked a little nervously.

"*Oui*, pearls *convenable* for mourning," Yvette replied. "Mean 'tears.' "

Pandia looked at her apprehensively as she went on:

"*Mais si quelqu'un me donnait des perles*, I not cry but jump for joy! Do not lose, *M'mselle*, they cost *Milor' beaucoup d'argent!*"

"I am sure they did!" Pandia exclaimed.

Finally when a footman knocked on her door to announce that the carriage was waiting, Yvette took from the wardrobe a coat of black astrakhan which fitted at the waist and swung out over her gown.

It had a huge collar of chinchilla and a little round muff of the same fur for her hands.

Finally, to complete the *ensemble* a small hat made of black velvet to match the trimming on her gown and decorated with black plumes was perched on top of her head.

"I am sure I look too smart!" Pandia said apprehensively. "And should I not have a veil?"

"What *Madame* wear is fine," Yvette assured her. "Veil hide pretty face."

Pandia remembered then that crêpe veils would be worn only by the widow, sisters, and daughters of the Duke, if he had any.

At the same time, because she was unused to such fantastic and glamorous clothes, she felt very self-conscious as she walked down the staircase and into the Hall.

She was relieved when the servants in attendance did not stare at her but only hurried to open the front door.

Two footmen rolled a red carpet down the steps and another footman helped her into the carriage and placed a sable rug over her knees.

Like yesterday, there was a foot-warmer for her feet and a satin cushion at her back.

The Butler and the footmen bowed as the carriage drove away.

It was different from the one she had travelled in with Selene, smaller but lightly sprung, and as soon as the four horses started moving out of London she realised they were travelling very fast.

She remembered that the Duke lived beyond Windsor Castle, and Yvette had reckoned it would not take her more than an hour-and-a-half to get to the Church where the Funeral was taking place.

But they had allowed a little more time, to be on the safe side, and as they reached the open country Pandia realised that it had been a wise precaution.

The sky was grey and overcast and it was a very cold day.

Snow had fallen in the night and there were a few flakes floating gently down now, which she thought might easily, if it grew worse, slow the horses and make her late.

It was important not to draw attention to herself, even though she realised that as Selene she was of importance.

She was therefore thankful when they drew up outside a grey stone Church a quarter-of-an-hour before the Funeral was due to begin.

There were a number of men in frock-coats standing in the porch and she knew they must be ushers.

She was therefore not surprised when one of them, a middle-aged man, held out his hand and said:

"How kind of you, Countess, to come in your husband's place. He wrote and told me he would be in France."

"He was very sorry he could not be present," Pandia
said in reply.

"Let me show you to your seat," the usher suggested.

She entered the Church to find it nearly full and was
aware as she walked up the aisle that all the people
turned their heads to look at her.

She was not surprised, after what Selene had said, to
find herself in the front pew, and was aware that the
pew on the other side of the aisle was being kept for the
late Duke's nearest relatives.

There was nobody else in her pew, and finding a card
with the Earl's name on it she realised that she was
sitting one place away from the aisle on her left. On her
right the name on the card was "The Marquis of
Orlestone."

She knelt down to pray, making a very fervent prayer
that she would not make any mistakes and that perhaps
if Selene was pleased with her she would wish sometimes,
even if secretly, to see her again.

Then as she sat back she was aware that on her left
nearest to the aisle there was now sitting an elderly
man wearing the uniform of a Lord Lieutenant, and on
the other side was a much younger man.

She turned her face to look at him and was aware that
he was staring at her with an expression of undisguised
admiration.

He was very good-looking in a somewhat unusual
manner, was tall and broad-shouldered, and Pandia
thought that in some way she could not describe he
looked something like her father.

As they looked at each other the man smiled and
said:

"Shall we introduce ourselves? I see you are repre-
senting your husband. I am Silvester Stone, represent-
ing my father."

He spoke in a very low voice that was almost a
whisper, and because she felt there was no need for her
to say anything, Pandia merely smiled at him.

"I hate Funerals!" Lord Silvester Stone said, "as I am

sure you do. I hope when I die I am thrown into the sea or perhaps down a volcano! A far better way of disposing of a dead body!"

The way he spoke made Pandia want to laugh, but because she was afraid somebody would notice and think it very out-of-place, she said:

"Please. . .do not make me laugh. I am sure everybody would be very. . .shocked!"

"They are not worrying about you," Lord Silvester Stone said, "but wondering what the deceased has left them. Nobody thinks of anything else at a Funeral!"

Because of the laughter in his voice and the twinkle in his eyes, Pandia had great difficulty in preventing herself from laughing.

Thinking it would be more proper, she turned her face away from him, and picking up the printed Service-sheet which had been handed to her at the entrance to the Church she opened it to see the usual familiar hymns: "Abide with Me" and "Onward, Christian Soldiers."

However, she was aware as she did so that Lord Silvester's eyes were on her face.

Then, although she told herself it was ridiculous, she felt herself blushing.

It was a relief when the choir came in, followed by the coffin, which was set down in the Chancel.

As the Service started and Pandia knelt to pray, Lord Silvester said in a voice only she could hear:

"You are beautiful! When I first looked at you I thought I must be dreaming and you had stepped down out of one of the stained-glass windows."

Pandia pretended she was not listening, and he went on:

"No, that is wrong! You are not a Christian Saint. I am sure they never looked like you! You have come down from Olympus, and I am just wondering which goddess you are when you are at home."

Because what he said was so apt, Pandia's lips twitched,

and as if she could not help herself she turned for one
swift moment to look at him, then looked away again.

"Your eyes are fantastic!" Lord Silvester said as the
Clergyman droned on pontifically in prayer.

Then as they rose, Pandia managed to say:

"Please. . .I am sure the people behind us are. . .
horrified at the way you are. . .behaving."

"You are coming back to the Castle after this is
over?"

She gave a little nod of her head.

"Then I will talk to you there."

He did not speak for the rest of the Service, but she
was vividly conscious of him standing beside her.

There was something about him, she thought, that
would make it impossible for anybody not to be aware
of his presence.

She knew it was the vibrations which came from his
personality, which was something she had often discussed with her father.

"Do you think," she had asked him once, "that if you
and I had suddenly met in a field or on a mountain-side
Buddha or Mohammed or perhaps even Jesus, we would
have been aware that they were different from anybody
else?"

"Of course," her father had replied. "The vibrations
that came from them must have been unmistakable."

"Vibrations?" Pandia had questioned.

"The magnetic rays, or what the Greeks expressed as
'shafts of light,' coming from the solar plexus of their
heroes and their gods."

Pandia remembered that she had seen drawings of
these, and her father had continued:

"Then the Christians transferred them to the heads of
their Saints, calling them halos. They are what we all
give out to a greater or lesser degree, from what we call
our souls, and it is the way our spirit speaks to the
world."

Pandia felt now that she could feel these rays, or
vibrations, coming from Lord Silvester towards her.

She could not help wondering if he felt the same from her, then thought she was being ridiculous.

It was only because she was so inexperienced and had met so few people that she should think of such things.

At the same time, she always remembered what her father had told her, and she was sure not only that it was her love for him which had made her think that he gave out very strong vibrations, but that they also made everybody who came in contact with him think of him as an unusual and interesting person.

"Yer father, Miss Pandia, may not 'ave been an Englishman," one of the farmers had said at his Funeral, "but to us 'e was always a real gentleman, and Oi can't say fairer than that."

Pandia had known it was the highest acclaim they could pay her father.

The women in the village had expressed their feelings differently.

"There's never been, dearie, a man as charmin' as yer Dad," they said. " 'E 'ad a way with 'im, that 'e 'ad, and ye takes after 'im—no doubt about that!"

Because she had known so few men of their own class with whom to compare her father, Pandia had sometimes wondered if he really was as unusual as she felt he was.

But her mother, who had loved him with her whole heart, had said:

"How could I have resisted your father? Whenever he looked at me I felt as if he drew me to him like a magnet. When finally he confessed that he loved me and asked me to run away with him, I did not even hesitate."

"It was very brave of you, Mama."

"No, darling, it was selfish, because I hurt my father and mother and my brothers, but it was my one chance of happiness. . .I knew that without your father I would never know the most precious and perfect thing in the world, which is love!"

"Papa certainly was magnetic," Pandia told herself as the coffin was carried by six men down from the Chancel towards the West Door, "but why should I feel that the man sitting next to me is the same?"

She told herself that she must be mistaken as, following the relatives from the pew on the other side of the aisle, they walked out side by side.

"Rather a wedding than all this pomp and circumstance for somebody who cannot enjoy it," Lord Silvester remarked.

Again Pandia wanted to laugh, but because she thought she should behave in a more circumspect way, she looked straight ahead of her, her hands clasped together inside her muff.

The Duke was to be buried in the family vault, which was just outside the West Door.

The relations gathered round for the last part of the Burial Service, and as they did so Pandia realised that there were not very many of them.

There was a very old woman who leant on a stick, and two or three quite young girls who she supposed were grandchildren or even great-grandchildren. The rest were mostly middle-aged or elderly men who stood bare-headed in the sharp biting wind with the snow-flakes lying on their shoulders.

The snow was blown onto her face, and it was so cold that Pandia shivered.

Then she felt Lord Silvester take her arm and draw her back towards the door of the Church.

"No, please," she said quickly, "I cannot. . .leave until it is. . .over."

"My mother always used to say," Lord Silvester replied, "that one Funeral in the winter breeds a host of others, and there is no point in your getting pneumonia."

"I do not think I shall do that."

"Well, perhaps I shall, and I certainly have no intention of catching a streaming cold and coughing and spluttering for the next few weeks."

Still holding her by the arm, he drew her through

the side-door by which they had entered, saying as he did so:

"We will go back to the Castle, and if our relatives had any sense they would not have allowed Lady Anne to come out on a day like thas."

"Lady Anne?" Pandia questioned.

"The Duke's sister who lived with him. She is eighty-seven, and far too old to be here, at least on her own feet!"

Lord Silvester's eyes were twinkling as he spoke, and because it seemed impossible to protest at what he was doing, Pandia let him draw her down the short path to where the carriages were waiting.

"May I travel with you?" he asked. "I will tell my carriage to follow us."

He helped her in, and then without waiting for her to reply he told the footman to wait while he gave instructions to his own servants.

He was away only for about a minute before he returned, stepped in beside Pandia, and pulled half the fur rug over his knees.

The horses moved off and he turned to her to say:

"Well, are you going to answer my question?"

"What question?"

"Which goddess are you?"

"My name is Pandia!"

Even as she spoke Pandia was aware that, bemused by Lord Silvester, she had made a terrible mistake.

Quickly she said to cover it up:

"That is what my father always. . .called me, but everybody knows me by. . .my other name. . .which is Selene."

"I never fancied her particularly," Lord Silvester replied. "She was far too promiscuous, and it was most unfair of her to get poor Endymion condemned to eternal sleep."

Pandia laughed, no longer trying to repress the laughter that had been bubbling inside her all through the Church Service.

"But 'Pandia' was a very different 'cup of tea,' " he went on, "and I remember she was 'remarkable for her beauty among the immortals.' "

Pandia stared at him.

"How can you know that? How are you so knowledge-able about Greek gods and goddesses?"

"It is a subject which interests me enormously," Lord Silvester replied, "and incidentally the gods have been kind, for I have found it very lucrative."

Pandia stared at him. Then she said:

"Stone! You cannot be J. Stone?"

"You have heard of me?"

"Of course I have! I adored *Forgotten Tongues*. And Papa also was thrilled by it and thought it was the most interesting book that had ever been written on the forgotten languages."

Now Lord Silvester stared at her.

"Are you telling me that you have read it too?"

"I enjoyed every word of it! It is the only book I have ever read that made Sanscrit seem understandable, and what you wrote about the Greeks helped Papa enor-mously with the translation he was doing at the time."

"Translation?" Lord Silvester exclaimed. "What is your father's name?"

"Micklos Hunyadi."

Lord Silvester gave a cry and reaching out took her hand in his.

"Now I understand why, the moment I saw you, or rather the second moment, I thought you were from Olympus! Only a Grecian goddess could have a straight little nose like yours!"

"You have read Papa's books?"

"I have read every one of them. What is he writing at the moment?"

Pandia looked away from him.

"Papa is. . .dead!"

She was just about to add that he died last week, when she remembered hastily that in that case she should be wearing deeper mourning than she was at the moment, which undoubtedly would not include a coat trimmed with chinchilla.

"I am sorry," Lord Silvester said, "not only because you have lost him, but because every word he wrote was like a light in a very dark world."

Pandia gave a deep sigh.

"How can you. . .understand?" she asked, then added: "But of course, when I think of what you have written, it is obvious that you can."

She remembered her father sending for *Forgotten Tongues* and saying:

"It is extravagant of me, but I could not resist this book when I heard it had been published. I read it all last night and found it impossible to put down. I know you will feel the same."

Pandia had loved every word.

It was all that her father tried to convey from the Greek, and J. Stone, whoever he might be, had translated the Vedas from the Sanskrit, making many things clear that she had not understood before.

Also by some brilliant research of his own he had discovered fragments of the Egyptian Book of the Dead, which her father had said had been lost since the time of the Pharaohs.

She felt as if every word sparkled like a jewel, and she had read it and reread it.

Just as it had helped her father with his translations of the Greek, so it had helped her to help him.

"I never thought I would ever meet you!" she said aloud.

"And I never thought you existed," Lord Silvester replied.

Because there was an intense note in his voice and Pandia was suddenly aware that he was still holding her hand, she quickly took it from him and put it back into her muff.

"What was your father writing before he died?" Lord Silvester asked.

"His book is not quite finished."

"Will you finish it?"

"I am going to try."

"I think you should let me help you."

Pandia was just about to say this would be the most wonderful thing that could happen, when she remembered that after today she would never see Lord Silvester again.

Without replying, she turned her head to look out through the window and exclaim:

"The snow is getting heavier!"

"Very much heavier," Lord Silvester agreed. "Have you come from London?"

"Yes, and I have to return there."

"It may be impossible."

"I am sure it will be all right," Pandia said, "but I must get away as soon as I possibly can."

He did not protest but merely said:

"Tell me more about your father's work. I have often wanted to meet him, but I have not been in England very often these past years."

"Where have you been?"

Pandia asked the question eagerly.

Then as he started to tell her of his travels, she realised with surprise that they had reached the Castle.

It was difficult to see what it looked like outside because now the snow was falling thicker and faster than it had before.

Inside, however, it was exactly what she thought the Castle of a Duke should be.

In the huge Hall there was an immense fireplace of carved marble in which one massive log of wood was burning.

There were suits of armour against the panelled walls and a number of tattered flags that must once have been captured in battle.

The Butler suggested that Pandia might like to go upstairs, and when she reached the very large, impressive bedroom there were two maids to assist her to remove her coat, and a silver basin filled with hot water in which to wash her hands was brought in.

The bed was a mediaeval oak four-poster with deep carvings, and through the diamond-paned casements she could see the white snow falling and relentlessly obliterating the garden and the park.

"It's nasty weather, M'Lady," one of the maids said to her, "and those who were at the Funeral'll find it hard to get home."

"I hope not," Pandia replied. "I have to return to London."

The elderly housemaid who had spoken to her pressed her lips together.

"I doubt if Your Ladyship'll reach London tonight. The horses won't see their way through snow like this."

"I am sure you are wrong."

Then, thinking that like all servants she was merely dramatising the situation, Pandia quickly went downstairs and was not surprised to find Lord Silvester waiting for her in the Hall.

Chapter Four

Gathered in the Baronial Dining-Hall were about thirty-five people, most of whom, Pandia saw at a glance, were very old.

Two or three others arrived after she had come downstairs, and as they chose what they wished to eat from a side-table groaning with food, she was thankful that nobody seemed to wish to talk to her.

"Suppose you sit down," Lord Silvester said, "and I will tell the servants to bring you what I think you would like."

"Thank you," Pandia replied.

She was over-awed at the enormous choice there was of great sides of roast beef, chicken, game, a boar's head, and innumerable other dishes about which she had only read in books or heard described by her mother.

Because it appeared that it was not known how many would be coming to the Castle, there were a number of small round tables in the Dining-Hall, and when everybody was seated there were at least half-a-dozen empty.

As Lord Silvester sat down beside her he was obviously aware of what she was thinking, and he said:

"Everybody with any sense has gone straight home from the Church. The snow is growing steadily heavier, and unless you have a celestial chariot waiting for you, you will have to stay here for the night."

Pandia started and said:

"I cannot do that. I have to get back."

"Why?"

Then before she could reply he added in a cynical tone:

"I imagine, as your husband is in Paris, some ardent swain is waiting for you, and who shall blame him if he is impatient?"

"There is nobody like that!"

Pandia spoke so positively that he looked at her quizzically.

"You can hardly expect me to believe there are not dozens, if not hundreds, of men kneeling at your feet and extolling your beauty."

Because it sounded so ridiculous, Pandia laughed before she answered:

"Everything you are saying is. . .untrue."

Then she realised it was what Selene would expect, and she was sure that besides Prince Ivor she had a number of admirers who might be exactly as Lord Silvester had described.

Because she did not want to talk about herself, she said:

"Tell me who everybody is. I feel I have been rather rude in not talking to anybody but you."

"That is exactly what I want you to do," he said, "and as Lady Anne has very wisely gone upstairs, this lot, as far as I can see, are of no great importance."

He spoke vaguely, and Pandia said:

"I expect really you do not know them yourself, as you have been abroad so much."

He smiled.

"I confess I am out of touch with my relatives, and although the Duke was not only my father's cousin but also my Godfather, I am not expecting to benefit from his Will."

"Why not? It is usual for Godparents to leave their Godchildren something."

"His Grace disliked the way I lived," Lord Silvester answered.

"That is what I want to hear about."

"I would much rather talk about you."

"Anything I could tell you would be very, very dull beside what you have achieved. When will your next book be published?"

"In two days' time!"

"Oh, no! How exciting! What is it called?"

"I shall tell you nothing about it until I can bring it to you and lay it as a tribute at your feet."

"No, please, tell me now!" Pandia pleaded.

As she spoke she had the uncomfortable feeling that she was stepping into deep water as far as Selene was concerned.

If he really brought his book to Selene, thinking he was giving it to her, he would undoubtedly be astonished to find that her sister knew practically nothing about the Greeks and had always been bored by what her father had tried to teach her.

'It is all a mistake,' Pandia thought to herself, 'but how could I have known, how could I have guessed for one moment, that J. Stone, of all people in the world, would be sitting next to me at the Funeral?'

"What is worrying you?" Lord Silvester asked.

"How do you know I am. . .worried?"

"Your eyes tell me that you are very worried and that something is upsetting you. I want you to tell me about it."

"You are mistaken," Pandia said quickly. "I am worrying about the snow and how I shall get back to London. Otherwise, I assure you, I am delighted to have met you."

She spoke in a light manner, as she thought Selene would have done, and he said:

"There is something wrong! Now you are on the defensive and trying to erect barriers between us, which is something it is impossible for you to do, as you must be aware."

"I. . .I do not know what you are. . .saying."

"Look at me."

Because he commanded her to do so, and without

really thinking, she raised her eyes to his. Then in some unaccountable fashion it was impossible to look away.

"You are just not real!" he said very quietly. "You are what I was searching for all the time I was in Greece."

The way he spoke made Pandia feel a very strange sensation in her breast which she had never known before.

She felt that he was hypnotising her in a magical way and it would be impossible to escape.

Then a footman at her side asked: "Champagne, M'Lady?" and the spell was broken.

Pandia refused, but Lord Silvester said:

"Have a little. It will warm you after the cold of the Churchyard."

"I think it is you who are feeling the cold. When did you come home?"

"I arrived back from India a week ago."

"Then of course you feel the cold, and you must be very careful to wrap up."

"Are you taking care of me?" Lord Silvester asked.

It flashed through Pandia's mind that it was something she would like to do, but she answered again in what she thought was the way Selene would have spoken:

"I expect there are a great many lovely ladies only too willing to do that!"

"I can promise you truthfully that none of them is as lovely as you!"

"You are very flattering, and although I was called after one of the goddesses, I assure you that I am very human, with, I am afraid, a great many human failings."

"I shall look forward to discovering what they are."

There was an intense note in his voice, and Pandia felt once again that strange sensation within her.

"I am sure now I should be leaving," she said quickly, "but before I go I should like, as she is my hostess, to meet Lady Anne."

Lord Silvester pushed back his chair.

"I will go to find out if it is possible for you to speak to her," he said.

He walked away and immediately an elderly woman rose from a nearby table to take his place.

"I know you are the Countess of Linbourne," she said. "I am a second-cousin of poor dear Rudolph, and therefore am a distant relative of your husband."

"I am so sorry he could not be present today," Pandia said politely.

"It was kind of you to represent him," the woman said. "I hope you will not have too difficult a journey going back to London. Fortunately, we live on the Estate, and so does nearly everybody else here."

She looked round the room and added:

"Lord Granville, who represented the Queen, insisted on returning to Windsor as soon as the Funeral was over. So, I noticed, did the Lord Lieutenant who was sitting next to you. He had quite some way to go to the other end of the County."

Pandia began to grow nervous.

"If the snow is so bad," she said, "I really must leave immediately!"

"I think you would be wise to do so."

Pandia rose to her feet. Then the Duke's cousin, as if she wanted to show her off, introduced her to several other people in the room.

They all shook their heads when she said she was returning to London, and she found that it was true that they all lived locally, either on the Estate or within a mile or so of the Castle.

She was getting more worried than she had been before when Lord Silvester came back into the Dining-Room.

"Lady Anne would be delighted to see you," he said. "She is upstairs in her *Boudoir*, but she did not feel well enough to meet many people. She is also very upset by her brother's death."

"I can understand that," Pandia said.

They walked side by side into the Hall, but before Pandia turned towards the stairs she said to the Butler:

"Will you please order my carriage? I must leave as soon as I have seen Her Ladyship."

Then she walked up the broad stairway, very conscious of the man walking by her side, and at the same time looking round because this was her one opportunity to see the Castle.

"Tell me about the paintings," she said as they reached the long corridor at the top of the stairs.

"They want cleaning!" Lord Silvester replied.

Pandia laughed and said:

"That is not the right answer, and I really am curious!"

"I would like to show you the Rajput miniatures at Mysore," Lord Silvester said. "This last trip was the first time I had seen them myself, and they are very beautiful."

"Papa has talked about them," Pandia replied. "He also told me about the wonderful ruins at Karnak, Pompeii, and of course Delphi, but they are places of which I can only dream and never see."

As she looked at him she saw the surprise in his eyes and realised that once again she had made a mistake.

"Why not?" he asked. "Surely your husband intends to take you abroad? And all these places are much easier to reach than they used to be."

Because she was so frightened at having said something so foolish, Pandia did not reply, and to her relief Lord Silvester stopped outside one of the doors in the corridor.

"I must be very quick," she said, "otherwise I shall never get back to London."

He opened the door and she found herself in a *Boudoir* which was very different from Selene's.

On a couch beside a brightly burning fire sat Lady Anne, and at her back were satin cushions which were faded with age, as was everything else in the room, and which seemed as old as she was.

Lady Anne had taken off the black bonnet with its

crêpe veil which she had worn in the Church, and now her white hair, which was rather sparse on her head, was a little untidy.

She had a thick woollen shawl in an unbecoming shade of grey over her shoulders, and she looked, Pandia thought, rather like one of the old women in the village whom she had regularly visited.

She held out her hand, and when she took Lady Anne's blue-veined one in hers, she realised how cold she was.

"It was very kind of you to come, my dear," Lady Anne said. "It is such a long way from London in this terrible weather."

"My husband was so sorry that he had to be in Paris," Pandia said gently.

"I am sorry not to have seen George," Lady Anne answered, "but I know how busy and important he is, and of course he is not getting any younger. You must take care of him."

"I will try," Pandia replied.

"Silvester tells me you are going back to London. I only hope the roads will be passable, but perhaps it would be wiser for you to stay the night."

"Oh, no," Pandia said quickly. "It is very kind of you, but I cannot do that."

"If the road is impassable, turn round and come back. There is plenty of room for you here."

"You are very kind," Pandia said, "but I am quite certain it will not be as bad as all that. Good-bye, and thank you very much for a delicious luncheon."

"I am glad you enjoyed it," Lady Anne said. "The Chefs have been working very hard, for most people want something to cheer them up after a burial."

"That is true, Cousin Anne," Lord Silvester said, speaking for the first time. "I will tell the Chefs later how much we enjoyed what they provided."

"Yes, do that, dear boy," Lady Anne said, "I know they will appreciate it. It has been difficult these days, while poor Rudolph has been ill for so long, to keep them interested in their work when we have not been able to entertain."

Pandia thought that what she was saying was rather touching.

She had noticed while they were talking that the room, in which the lights had not been lit, seemed to be growing darker, and the snow outside was falling more heavily than before.

"I really must be going," she said quickly. "Good-bye, Lady Anne, and thank you again."

"Good-bye, my dear. Be very careful of yourself and do not hesitate to turn back if the snow is too bad."

"It is very kind of you."

She walked towards the door and behind her heard Lord Silvester say:

"I will see the Countess off, Cousin Anne, but I will come back later and talk to you."

As he joined Pandia outside in the corridor she asked:

"Are you staying here?"

"I have arranged to stay tonight," he answered, "but I am going up to London tomorrow, God willing and the weather permitting."

"I suppose to see your book the day before it is published."

"I have a number of them to sign," Lord Silvester replied, "and you shall have the first."

An idea came to her, and she said a little hesitatingly:

"Would it be. . .possible for you to. . .bring it to me. . .tomorrow?"

"Tomorrow?"

"I may be. . .going away the next day. . .and I would like to. . .take it with me."

"Will you be away for long?"

"I do not know."

"Then I shall certainly bring you my book tomorrow."

Pandia felt somehow it was quite wrong, but her heart leapt at his promise.

She wondered what Selene would say if she knew

that Pandia had entertained somebody at Grosvenor Square in her absence.

Then Pandia told herself it would be far more complicated for Lord Silvester to present his book to Selene when she had not the slightest idea what it was all about.

"Perhaps," she suggested quickly, "you could come to tea?"

"That is an invitation I have no intention of refusing," Lord Silvester said, "and you know how much I will be looking forward to it."

He was speaking to her in a manner which not only made her feel shy, but it was impossible for her to look at him as she went slowly down the staircase.

She had expected, since she had said she was leaving, that her coat and muff would be waiting for her in the Hall.

The Butler, however, came forward as she reached the last step.

"I've sent to the stables, M'Lady, and your coachman says he's sorry, but it's quite impossible for Your Ladyship to reach London this evening. The snow's coming down so thick he can't see his hand in front of his face!"

Pandia turned to look at Lord Silvester.

"Are you sure that is right?" she asked.

"I warned you," he said, "and to risk an accident, which could easily happen driving blindly in weather like this, would be exceedingly foolish."

"I'm sure, M'Lady," the Butler said, "you'd be more comfortable here, and the weather may clear up by tomorrow morning."

Pandia looked helpless and Lord Silvester said:

"Her Ladyship has already suggested that the Countess should stay if the weather is too bad. Will you tell Mrs. Whiteley to prepare a room for her? I am sure she can provide anything Her Ladyship needs."

"I am sure she can, M'Lord," the Butler replied.

"Very good, Bates. Now I think we will go and sit in the Blue Drawing-Room if there is a fire there."

"I anticipated Your Lordship would want to be in the Small Library this evening," the Butler replied, "and as there has been a fire there all day, it'll be warmer for Her Ladyship."

"Very well, the Small Library it is," Lord Silvester agreed.

He put his hand under Pandia's elbow and led her across the Hall and down the passage hung with paintings and ancient weapons, and she felt again that there was everything she expected to find in a Castle.

The Small Library seemed to her a very large room, and as they entered it Lord Silvester said:

"Another time I would like to show you the Big Library, which contains over twenty thousand books, but as it will certainly be very cold, I think we should stay here and be comfortable."

There was a leather-covered sofa in front of an enormous fireplace in which the logs were burning brightly, and over the mantelpiece was a large oil-painting titled *The Judgement of Paris*.

The subject had been painted by many artists, but in this particular painting Pandia thought all three goddesses were exceptionally beautiful and Paris looked strong, masculine, and very much a man.

Lord Silvester followed the direction of her eyes and said:

"As you must be well aware, none of them are as beautiful as you, and that includes Aphrodite!"

"You are making me very conceited," Pandia replied, "and I am still rather perturbed at not being able to return to London as I intended."

"Who is waiting for you there?"

"Only the servants, who I presume will. . .guess what has. . .happened to me."

"Do you expect me to believe that?"

"I cannot think why it should concern you one way or the other," Pandia replied.

She had sat down on the sofa which was on one side of the fireplace and he sat beside her.

"You know that is a ridiculous answer," he said. "I am concerned with anything that concerns you, and do not pretend that you are not aware of it."

Because he was very near to her and she was so acutely conscious of him, she found it difficult to know what to reply and instead just stared into the fire.

"There are a million things I want to say to you," Lord Silvester said unexpectedly, "and yet now they fade into insignificance, and all I can think of is that you are here, I can look at you, and you are no longer a part of my dreams."

She looked at him, then quickly looked away again.

"When we. . .arrived," she said in a hesitating little voice, "you were. . .just going to tell me about your. . . journeys abroad. That is what I want to. . .hear about."

"There is plenty of time for that," Lord Silvester said. "All I can think of now is that you are lovelier than I ever imagined anybody could be, and when I sat down beside you in the Church I felt as if I had climbed to the top of the Himalayas and found you waiting for me."

Because Pandia found that what he was saying had a strange effect on her, she said quickly:

"Please. . .you must not. . .talk to me like this. . .you must be sensible."

Lord Silvester laughed.

"What is sensible? To discuss the weather and the crops, or to talk about ourselves? You know quite well it is impossible for us to talk about anything else."

"But. . .we must not. . .you should not. . ." Pandia tried to say.

He laughed again very softly and rather tenderly.

"Oh, my dear," he said, "you are so sweet, so different from what I thought you would be. When I look at you I am astounded by your loveliness! When I talk to you I am bewildered because, while I know who you are, you are still like a little girl on the threshold of life who knows nothing about the world and is looking at it with puzzled, innocent eyes."

Pandia drew in her breath.

Then, as if he was thinking it out for himself, Lord Silvester went on:

"I suppose it is because you are living in two worlds: the smart, sophisticated world in which I have been told you shine, and the world which I feel belongs to me, and which is the world your father knew."

"That is the world which interests me," Pandia said, "so. . .please. . .tell me what I want to. . .know, in case I never have the. . .opportunity of talking to you of it. . .again."

She thought as she spoke that she must treasure everything he told her as something to remember when she was back at Little Barford and, as far as the Social World was concerned, had ceased to exist.

As if he understood what she wanted he said:

"I will talk to you about anything you like, but make no mistake, this is the first conversation of many. I have so much to share with you; so much which I feel only you will understand."

"Why do you say. . .that?" Pandia asked.

"Because up until now I have been entirely alone," he said. "I have enjoyed my life, it has been a great adventure, but I have never had anybody really interested with whom to discuss my findings, or to share in my excitement when I discover something that has been hidden or forgotten for thousands of years."

"How do you. . .know that I shall. . .understand?"

In answer he took her hand from her lap and held it in both of his.

She felt something like a streak of lightning run through her because he was touching her.

He must have been aware of it, because he said:

"Has anybody else ever made you feel like that?"

He did not wait for her reply, but said gently:

"I feel the same. It has never happened to me before, and I am quite certain it will never happen again!"

Because she was frightened, Pandia took her hand from his.

"I am. . .waiting," she said in a voice that sounded strange even to herself, "for you to tell me about . .India. Is that the last. . .country you. . .visited?"

Very quietly he started to tell her of the Rajput paintings he had seen in Udaipur, and of some old manuscripts he had discovered there which, when he translated them, were poems of such beauty that everybody who listened to them had been astonished.

"And they are in your book?" Pandia asked.

"Not in the one which is being published now," he replied, "but in my next book, the book which I want you to help me with."

"How can I do that when I have never been to India?"

"It also includes a great deal about Greece, and I have some ancient parchments which have only recently been unearthed in a long-forgotten Temple, and which I have not yet translated."

Pandia clasped her hands together.

"If only Papa were alive!"

"I wish he were! I would certainly have asked him to help me," Lord Silvester said, "but I have the feeling that you will do it as well as he would."

Pandia was just about to reply that nothing would be more exciting when she remembered that, while she might receive his book tomorrow, after that she could never see him again.

She asked him question after question and they went on talking.

Only when the Butler came in to pull the curtains did she realise that it was now tea-time and she had been alone for over two hours with a man, which was something she had never experienced in her life before.

The Butler and two footmen brought in the tea, which involved a magnificent array of silver, besides scones, sandwiches, hot toast, a large fruit-cake, and several plates of small ones.

"Enough," Lord Silvester said, "for a Regiment of soldiers!"

"I. . .I am really not. . .hungry," Pandia protested.

"You must eat," he insisted, "otherwise the Chefs, as Lady Anne said, who have nobody to cook for and are very frustrated by it, will be disappointed."

Because he pressed her, Pandia ate some of the little fairy-cakes and found them delicious, but she noticed that Lord Silvester ate very little.

"You are cheating and thinking of your figure," she teased, "while making me stuff myself in a very greedy manner."

"I have always found it too much trouble to eat at regular intervals or to stop just because it is midday when I am busy doing something interesting."

"Mama said Papa always forgot to eat when he was immersed in his translations. What you need is a wife to look after you."

"That is something I have just begun to realise," Lord Silvester replied.

Once again he was looking at her in a way which made her feel shy.

The hours seemed to fly by until Pandia was aware that as dinner was at eight o'clock she should go upstairs to wash and tidy herself.

"When you come down I will see that Bates has the Silver Salon ready for you," Lord Silvester said. "It is a room I think you will appreciate, and where I particularly want to see you."

She did not have to ask the reason. She was aware of what he was thinking, and it made her blush.

As she walked up the stairs she wished that she could change into an evening-gown for dinner, knowing that because Lord Silvester was staying in the house he would have his evening-clothes with him.

The Housekeeper, Mrs. Whiteley, was waiting for her in a different room from the one which she had been shown when she had first arrived.

This was in another part of the Castle, and Pandia was sure it had been decorated later and was certainly not only very comfortable but very beautiful.

There was a painted ceiling, and instead of the heavy carved mediaeval bed she had seen before, there was a four-poster, carved and gilded, with curtains of Boucher blue trimmed with gold and silver fringes.

"What a lovely room!" she exclaimed.

"I thought you'd think so, M'Lady," Mrs. Whiteley replied. "It has been decorated in the last two years by Her Ladyship, who I suppose now I should refer to as 'Her Grace.'"

"I expect you mean the late Duke's daughter-in-law," Pandia said.

"That's right, M'Lady. The Marquis and Her Ladyship are in Australia at the moment, which is why they couldn't get home for the Funeral. We look forward to their return, and there'll be many improvements made in the Castle after that."

Looking round the room and remembering the contrast between this and Lady Anne's room, Pandia could understand that there was a great deal to be done.

Now as she moved towards the dressing-table she said:

"I am afraid you will have to find me a nightgown to wear tonight, as naturally I had no idea I should have to stay."

"I've been thinking about that, M'Lady, and it's no problem," Mrs. Whiteley replied. "Her Ladyship left everything here when she went to Australia, and as you are about the right size, although a trifle thinner, I wondered if you would like to borrow one of her gowns to wear for dinner this evening?"

The Housekeeper spoke a little nervously, as if she felt Pandia might be insulted at the suggestion, but instead she replied eagerly:

"Could I do that? I was just thinking how disappointing it would be to have to wear a day-gown while I eat what is sure to be a delicious meal."

"I'll bring some gowns for your inspection, M'Lady," Mrs. Whiteley said. "It'll be quite like old times to have a Lady to dress for dinner. Lady Anne always dines alone in her *Boudoir*."

"How long have the new Duke and Duchess been away?" Pandia asked.

"Nearly a year, M'Lady, but now they are on their way home and should be back in a month's time."

It was then, as Pandia started to undress, that her bath was brought into the room and set down in front of the fire, in the way her mother had always described.

It was a hip-bath, and as she washed in warm water that had been brought up in highly polished brass cans, she thought this was really an adventure, and she was enjoying every moment of it.

There had been nothing to frighten her at the Funeral, after all, and to have met a man whom her father had admired and whose books had delighted him more than any others was something she knew she would always treasure in her memory.

"I shall never see him again," she told herself, "but I will never, never forget him!"

She dried herself with an enormous, warm Turkish towel in front of the fire while Mrs. Whiteley brought her fresh under-clothes.

They were as beautiful as Selene's and heavily trimmed with lace, something which she had never possessed herself and never expected to feel next to her skin.

Then there was a choice between a white gown of crêpe trimmed with ruched chiffon or a black one of tulle spangled with jet.

They were both lovelier than anything Pandia had ever seen or possessed, and while she hesitated Mrs. Whiteley said:

"I didn't think you'd want anything in a colour, M'Lady. At the same time, as you've been in black all day, I'd like to see you in the white gown."

"Very well," Pandia replied, "and as I cannot wear them both, I should be delighted to borrow the white gown, if you are quite certain Her Grace will not mind."

"Her Grace is very generous in everything she does,"

Mrs. Whiteley replied. "She's His Grace's second wife, and not yet thirty, so her clothes are very young and fashionable, which here in the Castle we all enjoys to see."

Pandia was thinking how most of the people at the Funeral had seemed very old, and she could understand how a young Duchess would cheer them all up.

Although she had been too polite to say so, she had been surprised that the Duchess's gowns were so elegant.

She had been thinking that because the old Duke had been ninety when he died, it was unlikely that his successor would be a young man.

Then she wondered, while Mrs. Whiteley was arranging her hair, whether the new Duchess, like Selene, was finding her elderly husband boring and perhaps looking for a handsome Prince to make her happy.

Pandia told herself she was still shocked at the way Selene was behaving.

At the same time, she felt that if the Prince talked to Selene in the same way as Lord Silvester had been talking to her, she might find it difficult to remember that she was a married woman and expected to be staid and dignified like her elderly husband.

Mrs. Whiteley stood back from the dressing-table.

"What do you think of that, M'Lady?" she asked.

Pandia had been deep in her reverie as she was thinking of Selene and had not realised that Mrs. Whiteley had not only rearranged her hair in the same way that it had been when she arrived but had placed two white roses on top of her head.

"Her Ladyship sometimes wears egrets or ospreys," Mrs. Whiteley said, "but I thought the roses would be more attractive with this gown."

"I can see you are an artist, Mrs. Whiteley," Pandia said, and the Housekeeper looked quite coy at the compliment.

"I've often thought I'd like to try my hand, M'Lady, at decorating rooms or designing gowns, but then I've never had the opportunity."

"Perhaps one day your dreams will come true," Pandia said lightly. "It is what we all want."

"That's a fact, M'Lady. And now let's see how you look in the white gown. If you don't like it, there are plenty more to choose from, but I somehow don't picture you in a bright colour."

As she was fastening her into the gown, which fitted her surprisingly well, Pandia felt sure that Mrs. Whiteley had been right.

She looked very young in the white gown.

If Lord Silvester had thought of her as a girl on the threshold of a new and unknown world, that was exactly how she appeared now.

In the gas-light with which the Castle was lit, the red in her hair seemed like little tongues of fire, and the whiteness of her skin was accentuated by the softness of the chiffon which framed her shoulders.

"Your Ladyship looks lovely! Really lovely!" Mrs. Whiteley exclaimed.

There was a note of pride in her voice, as if she herself had produced a masterpiece, and Pandia smiled as she said:

"Thank you very much indeed! You have been exceedingly kind, and I am very grateful!"

"When you come upstairs, M'Lady, Emma'll be waiting to help you undress. She's a good girl and'll look after you."

"Thank you," Pandia said. "I shall not be late."

She walked slowly down the corridor, knowing with a feeling of delight that she had never worn such a beautiful gown.

She enjoyed the rustle of her silk petticoats and felt they made what was almost a "purring" sound over the carpet.

The gown, like the black one of Selene's, fitting tightly over the bodice, and the ruched chiffon swept out over the hem like the waves of the sea.

Round her neck she wore Selene's pearl necklace and her ear-rings.

They did not give her any look of sophistication, but again her youth and the translucence of the pearls seemed to blend with the clarity of her skin.

Bates, who was waiting for her at the bottom of the stairs, escorted her across the Hall.

Two footmen flung open a pair of double doors and she found herself in the Silver Salon.

She needed only one look at the crystal chandeliers with the lighted candles and a glimpse of white pillars picked out in silver and glistening Venetian mirrors to know why Lord Silvester had thought it was the right background for her.

She knew the light was all part of the light he found in Greece, which was the light of the gods, and perhaps the light too which flowed from them both.

He was standing at the far end of the Salon in front of an exquisitely carved mantelpiece.

He did not move as Pandia started to walk towards him, and as she felt his eyes watching her she felt very young, very unsure, and shy in a way she had never been shy before.

As she reached him he took her hand in his to say very softly:

"Oh, my dear, you are the moonlight itself, just as I knew you would be!"

Then as he kissed her hand, and she felt his lips warm and insistent against her skin, she felt herself quiver.

Chapter Five

"*W*here are you travelling next?" Pandia asked.

They had talked for hours, and the time had seemed to pass so swiftly that she had not asked Lord Silvester half the things she wanted to know.

"In a week or ten days," he replied, "I am going to Tafraout."

He saw the question in her eyes, and before she could speak he added:

"It is in the Ammein Valley in Southern Morocco, and is, I believe, one of the three most beautiful places in Africa and has never yet been seen by an Anglo-Saxon."

"How exciting for you!" Pandia exclaimed. "How I wish I could come with you!"

She spoke without thinking, then as she saw the strange expression in his eyes she blushed and said quickly:

"Nevertheless, I will dream about it, as I dream of other places which I shall never see."

Then as she felt once again that he might say that as her husband was rich he could afford to take her anywhere she wished to go, she added quickly:

"What is your book to be called?"

"I have not yet decided upon the title," he said, "but I think *Forbidden Places* would be appropriate."

"Forbidden?" she asked. "Where else is included?"

"Tibet was the most obvious," he replied, "and of course Mecca."

"You have been to Mecca? You have really been there?"

She knew that if any white man was discovered trying to enter the Holy of Holies of the Muslim world, he would be put to death, and she felt frightened at the risks Lord Silvester must have run.

"I found it a most interesting and enlightening journey," he said quietly.

Pandia was just about to ask him to tell her about it when she was aware that it was growing late.

Without thinking, almost as if the words came involuntarily to her lips, she said:

"I suppose we should go to bed."

She rose as she spoke and was surprised when Lord Silvester replied:

"I think that is an excellent idea!"

She had been expecting him to protest that he did not want her to leave him, and now she thought she must have behaved as Selene would never have done and overstayed her welcome.

Because she was embarrassed, she walked towards the door, and after a moment he followed her.

There was a night-footman in the Hall, who rose from a chair as soon as they appeared, and as Pandia reached the staircase she said to him:

"Good-night!"

"Good-night, M'Lady!"

She was aware that Lord Silvester was just behind her, and she thought it would perhaps seem strange if they walked upstairs together.

Standing on the bottom step, she held out her hand.

"Good-night, My Lord!" she said. "Thank you for the most interesting and exciting evening I have ever spent!"

He took her hand in his, and she felt his vibrations so strongly that they seemed almost to tingle up her arm.

Then hurriedly, because she was shy, she went up the stairs without looking back.

When she reached her bedroom she did not have to

ring the bell because Emma was already there waiting for her.

She was a young maid, which was why she was expected to stay up late at night, and was not talkative like Mrs. Whiteley.

Pandia spoke a few words to her, then was content to relapse into her thoughts, thinking that she had been very remiss in not leaving Lord Silvester at least an hour earlier.

Then she told herself that whatever he thought of her it was of no consequence.

After he had brought her his book as he had promised to do tomorrow afternoon, she would never see him again.

He would disappear into the unknown, and she would return to Little Barford and be completely forgotten.

It was a depressing thought. At the same time, because she was still thrilled by their conversation and the strange feelings he had aroused in her, for the moment she was not depressed or even apprehensive of the future.

She knew that once she returned home it would be impossible not to be afraid of the years in which there would be only Nanny to talk to, and nothing would happen except the slow passing of the seasons, one by one.

She would grow older, and doubtless not only her beauty would vanish but her brain would ossify without the stimulus of her father's presence and his translations to occupy her.

'I may be able to finish his book,' Pandia thought, 'but I doubt if I am competent enough on my own to start another.'

She remembered how Lord Silvester had offered to help her, and she could imagine nothing more perfect than that they should work together.

He would make the forgotten languages and places on which he was such an expert come alive.

"He is a very wonderful person!" she told herself as

she got into bed, and tried to think how grateful she
should be for having met him.

Then she thought:

'Even if I am never able to see him again, I shall
know what he is doing from his books.'

She knew, however, that it would never be the same
as being vividly aware that he was sitting beside her and
talking to her in his deep voice, the expression in his
eyes making her feel shy.

As Emma turned out the gas-lights there were only
two candles left on a table beside the bed.

"Good-night, M'Lady!" she said as she reached the
door.

"Good-night, Emma, and I am sorry to have kept you
up so late," Pandia replied.

"It's been a pleasure, M'Lady!"

The maid bobbed her a little curtsey, then left the
bedroom, closing the door quietly behind her.

Pandia lay back against the pillows.

She did not want to blow out the light because she
wanted to look at her bedroom and think it was the sort
of room in which she would never sleep again.

'Perhaps I could write a story about the Castle,' she
thought, 'where the heroine would sleep in this room,
meet the man of her dreams, marry him, and become
the Duchess of Dorringcourt.'

But she knew that even in her thoughts she was
cheating herself, and it was not the Duke of Dorringcourt
she was thinking about, but Lord Silvester.

"No Duke," she told herself, "could be more handsome and certainly no Duke could have the same
magnetism, or what Papa used to call 'shafts of light'
coming from him like one of the ancient Greeks."

Then, as if her thoughts of him had conjured him,
the door into the *Boudoir* opened and Lord Silvester
came into the room.

For a second Pandia thought she must be imagining
him.

He shut the door behind him and came towards her,

and she stared at him in astonishment, her eyes seeming to fill her whole face.

"Why. . .are you. . .here?" she managed to stammer as he reached the bed. "Y-you should not. . .come to my. . .room!"

There was a faint twist of Lord Silvester's lips as he stood looking at her with the red in her hair glinting like little flames from the light of the candles as it fell over her shoulders.

"We had not finished saying 'good-night' to each other," he said quietly.

He seated himself on the side of the bed, facing her. He was wearing a black robe with Chinese dragons embroidered on it in gold.

"I. . .I said good-night to. . .you," Pandia replied.

Because he was so close to her, her heart was beating in a strange manner and she was finding it difficult to speak.

"Not the way I want you to," Lord Silvester replied. "Besides, it was you who suggested *we* should go to bed!"

Pandia gave a little cry of horror.

"I did not. . .mean that. . .of course I did not mean. . .that!"

"Why not?"

As she could find no words in which to answer him, he said very quietly:

"Perhaps you will think it too soon, but we both know without words what we feel about each other, and we may never have an opportunity like this again."

"I. . .I do not know. . .what you are. . .saying to me," Pandia faltered.

She knew by the expression in his eyes that he did not believe her.

She was also acutely conscious that the nightgown she was wearing, which had belonged to the new Duchess, was, like Selene's diaphanous and very transparent.

Instinctively she pulled the sheet a little higher.

It was a defensive movement, and Lord Silvester said, and now there was a touch of surprise in his voice:

"You are very young. At the same time, you are married, and I cannot believe that you do not understand what I feel about you and how much I want you."

"You must not say. . .things like. . .that," Pandia said. "It is. . .wrong."

"You and I both know that to the Greeks love is never wrong," Lord Silvester replied, "and you and I, my adorable little goddess, are one with the gods."

He bent forward as he spoke, and before Pandia was really aware of what he was about to do, his arms went round her and his lips were on hers.

He took her by surprise.

Then as she knew that she must struggle against him and her hands moved to push him from her, his lips gave her a sensation she had never known existed.

It was like the vibrations which she felt from him, and yet it was far more intense, far more ecstatic.

She felt as if shafts of light were running through her, from his lips to her breasts, and from her breasts over her whole body until she could not breathe for the wonder of it.

His arms tightened and his mouth became more possessive, more demanding, more insistent.

While at the back of her mind Pania knew that she should struggle, she felt as if something within her which she could not control leapt like a flame towards him.

'I belong to him,' she thought. 'I am his!'

She felt as if he carried her up to the very pinnacle of Olympus, and, as he had said, they were no longer human but were gods and enveloped by a celestial light.

Lord Silvester raised his head.

"You *are* a goddess," he said, "for no human woman has ever made me feel like this, and I can only say that I love you!"

His voice was very deep and moving as he looked

down at her eyes shining in the candlelight, her lips trembling from his kisses, her face framed by her hair.

He thought that even a goddess could not look more lovely.

"I love you," he repeated, "and, darling, I want you as I know you want me!"

Then as his words brought her slowly back from the glory into which he had taken her, Pandia was suddenly aware of what he was saying.

With what was a superhuman effort she managed to find her voice.

"This is. . .wrong! Please. . .you must not. . .kiss me. . .again!"

"It is not a question of kissing you," Lord Silvester replied. "I want to make your beautiful, exquisite body mine, as your mind already is."

"No. . .no!" Pandia cried.

She put her hands flat against his chest to try to push him away from her.

As she touched him she was aware of his strength and how completely helpless she was.

"Why are you fighting me?" he asked. "What we have found, my precious, is so perfect that it would be a crime to deny it."

Pandia thought the same thing.

But although she did not know exactly what happened when a man made love to a woman, she knew it was something she must not allow, and it would be a sin if they were not married.

"Please. . .do not kiss. . .me," she pleaded.

Her voice was very weak and helpless, and she knew by the fire in his eyes that she merely excited him more.

"How can you stop me?" he asked.

Then he was kissing her again, kissing her with long, slow, passionate kisses that seemed to grow more demanding and more insistent until Pandia thought he held her completely captive.

It was impossible to think or be aware of anything except the shafts of light within her, which felt like tongues of fire flickering and growing stronger every minute his lips were on hers.

Then like a voice coming out of a mist she could hear Selene say:

"At least Papa gave me something! I certainly have fire in my blood."

As she thought of her sister, Pandia remembered how shocked she had been at her taking the Prince as her lover, and she knew that she too was behaving in a most reprehensible manner which would have horrified her mother.

With an effort that was almost like tearing away part of her body, she turned her head and took her mouth from Lord Silvester's.

"Please. . ." she begged. "Please. . .please listen to me. . .there is. . .something I have to. . .say to you."

"There is nothing to say," he replied passionately. "This is not a time for words, but for love!"

She felt his hand moving down the side of her body, and the warmth and strength of it through her night-gown made her aware of what he intended.

She struggled against him, then as he pulled away the sheet which covered her breasts she said frantically;

"You are. . .frightening me. . .please listen to me. . . please. . .please. . ."

Her voice sounded like that of a child who was really afraid, and it stopped Lord Silvester as nothing else could have done.

He looked down at her searchingly, then said in a different voice from the one he had used before:

"You *are* afraid. But why? I do not understand!"

"You are. . .frightening me. . .and while I am not quite. . .certain what you are. . .trying to do. . .I know it is. . .very wrong. . .and something Mama would have. . .considered wicked!"

Slowly Lord Silvester took his arms from her and sat up.

Although he had freed her, Pandia did not feel a sense of relief.

Instead she felt a loss, as if he had taken away from her something very precious.

Then she managed to say incoherently:

"Try to. . .understand. . .it is so difficult. . .but you must not. . .touch me."

"I have touched you!" Lord Silvester said. "And what is it I am to understand?"

He looked down into her eyes, which seemed to be pleading with him, and saw her put both her hands protectively over her breasts, as if it was a gesture of modesty to hide them from him.

His eyes searched her face. Then he said:

"If I did not know you were a married woman, I would have sworn this is the first time you have ever been kissed!"

Pandia's eyes flickered and for a moment her lashes were very long and dark against her pale cheeks.

Then Lord Silvester said sharply:

"Look at me and tell me the truth! Has any man ever possessed you?"

For a moment Pandia did not understand what he was asking, then forgetting everything except that the idea was so shocking, she said quickly:

"No. . .of course. . .not! How can you. . .think I would. . .do. . .anything. . ."

Even as she spoke and saw the expression on his face, her voice died and she realised she was speaking as herself and not as Selene.

"Is that true?" Lord Silvester asked. "How can I believe it?"

Then, suddenly afraid of what she had said and what he might be thinking, and shocked by the position in which she found herself, Pandia cried:

"Go away! You have. . .no right to come here. . .and ask me a lot of. . .questions. It is. . .late. . .and I want to go. . .to. . .sleep!"

As she spoke, she was so apprehensive about the

whole situation that tears came into her eyes and her voice broke.

Then Lord Silvester reached out and took her hand in his.

"I have upset you," he said, "and that is something I have no wish to do. I do not understand, in fact I find it completely bewildering, but we will talk about it tomorrow."

His fingers were somehow very comforting, but as if she was aware that she had somehow disappointed or failed him, she said hesitatingly:

"I. . .I am sorry. Tonight was so. . .wonderful!"

"If I have spoilt it for you I am sorry too, but you bewilder me, and I believed there was very little left in the world that could do that!"

Instinctively her fingers tightened on his.

"You are not. . .angry with me?"

He shook his head.

"No, not angry, just, as I say, bewildered, and I have no idea what I can do next."

"I shall. . .see you. . .tomorrow?"

"If you want to."

"Please. . .please come to see me and bring me your book. . .it will be something to remember when. . ."

She stopped and knew that once again she was being indiscreet.

He did not move. He merely sat looking at her as though he was imprinting her face on his mind.

Then his fingers tightened until they were painful as he said:

"I will leave now because you have asked me to, and because I would not force you to do anything you have no wish to do. At the same time, I suppose you know you have closed the gates of Paradise and left me outside?"

"I did not. . .wish to do that," Pandia said, "but. . .it is something I. . .have to do."

"Why?"

"I. . .I cannot tell you. . .that."

"I thought when we were talking downstairs that I could read your thoughts, and I was aware that you were reading mine. I believed it would be impossible for there to be any secrets between us."

Because Pandia had thought the same thing, she desperately wanted to tell him the truth, to explain who she was and why she was here.

Then she knew that she could not be so disloyal to Selene, for he might expose her deception to other people, with the result that Selene would be disgraced and perhaps even divorced by her husband.

The idea was so horrifying that Pandia thought with a sudden panic that perhaps she had already created in Lord Silvester's mind a suspicion that might reach out indefinitely to menace Selene's happiness and security.

"What is upsetting you?" he asked.

"Will you. . .promise," she replied, "on everything you hold. . .sacred that you will not. . .tell anybody what we have. . .talked about this evening. . .or that you. . .kissed me?"

"Do you really imagine I would do such a thing?" Lord Silvester asked, and now there was a touch of anger in his voice.

"I. . .I am sorry. . .forgive me," Pandia faltered, "but I am. . .frightened of a scandal. . .and of gossip. . . and. . ."

She paused, feeling for words.

"And your reputation in the Social World?"

Now there was definitely a cynical note in his voice, which Pandia had never heard before.

Because she could not help herself, she replied:

"No. . .it is not that. . .I cannot. . .explain. . .but I swear it is not. . .that."

"Why do you not trust me?" he asked. "There is of course no reason why you should, but you must be aware that the gods have brought us to each other, and this is not the first time we have met."

Pandia drew in her breath.

She knew he was speaking of reincarnation, in which her father had believed and so did she.

She knew they had met in other lives, and that was why she had been so vividly conscious of him the moment he had sat down in Church.

That too was the reason why, when he kissed her, she had known that it was the most perfect and wonderful thing that had ever happened to her and she belonged to him. She was his.

"I. . .believe that too," she said in a voice he could barely hear, "but we must not. . .think about it. . .we must. . .forget."

"Are you suggesting," Lord Silvester asked, "that after tomorrow you will be able to forget that I exist? That you will never think of me again?"

"I shall think of. . .you again," Pandia said, "but you must. . .forget me."

"Why should I do that?"

She realised that she could not answer him, and he said:

"I have searched the world for you, expecting to find you in Greece, or perhaps in one of the other strange places in which I have been. Then like a miracle I find you in a very ordinary English Church attending a Funeral!"

It sounded almost amusing, but Pandia could not smile.

She knew that while she had never looked for the man who was the other half of herself in such places as Lord Silvester had explored, she had sought for him in her dreams.

It was he who had always been in her mind when she and her father had talked of Olympus, of Delphi, and of the gods who had set aside their Divinity to take human guise.

Now she knew that it was Lord Silvester whom she had seen in her mind and felt with her heart, and to whom the light within her had reached out, although she had no idea he was a living man.

But now he was here, sitting beside her, holding her hand, and it flashed through her mind that she was being extremely foolish to refuse to let him love her as he wished to do.

She knew that if he did so, he would again carry her up to the peaks of Olympus, and as the celestial light covered them they would, as he had said, enter Paradise together.

As if he could feel exactly what she was thinking, he said in a very deep voice:

"You make it very hard for me, my little goddess, and yet I would cut off my right arm rather than hurt you in any way."

As he spoke he lifted her hand to his lips.

He kissed her fingers one by one, then turned them over and his mouth was on her palm.

She felt thrill after thrill flash through her as he did so, and then because once again the fire was flickering within her, without thinking or reasoning, she lifted her lips towards his.

He looked down at her, and as she waited for his kiss he drew a little nearer, but his lips did not touch hers.

Instead he said very quietly:

"I love and worship you, but I dare not touch you again. We may feel like gods, my darling, but tonight I am a man and you are slowly crucifying me."

He kissed the hand he was holding and very gently put it on her breast, then rose to his feet.

"Now that I have found you," he said, "make no mistake, I do not intend to lose you."

Without saying any more, he turned and walked towards the door through which he had come into the room.

As he reached it he looked back.

Only as she realised that he was really leaving her did Pandia make an inarticulate little murmur and move her hands as if she would reach out to hold on to him.

"I love you!" Lord Silvester said quietly. "Now go to

sleep. Remember that I love you, and as I think you love me—there is nothing either of us can do about it."

The door closed behind him and there was silence.

* * *

As Pandia dressed the following morning, Mrs. Whiteley brought her the good news that the weather had cleared and the coachman anticipated that once they were out on the main road they would be able to reach London without any difficulties.

"Her Ladyship would like to see you, M'Lady, before you leave," she said, "so if you come up after breakfast I will have everything ready for you."

"Thank you very much," Pandia said.

She had been relieved to find that there was a considerable amount of money in her hand-bag.

She was therefore able to tip both Mrs. Whiteley and Emma generously, and she knew she would have to give at least three sovereigns to the Butler.

Her mother had often told her that large tips were expected in the great houses where she had stayed as a girl.

But she was sure it was Yvette who had thought of putting so much money in the hand-bag which had been Selene's, as her sister would never have considered how little money she had of her own.

She took one last glance at herself in the mirror after Mrs. Whiteley had arranged her hair, then as she walked downstairs she knew with a frantic beating of her heart that she was both apprehensive and excited at the thought of seeing Lord Silvester again.

What had happened last night now seemed like a dream, and yet she knew she would never forget the wonder of his kisses.

She entered the Breakfast-Room, where she was shown by a footman, but to her disappointment he was not there.

Then as she thought that perhaps he might be down

later, she realised that the table was laid only for one
person.

"Good-morning, M'Lady!" the Butler said as he held
a chair for her.

Because she could not prevent herself from asking
the question, Pandia asked:

"Has His Lordship already breakfasted?"

"Yes, M'Lady, and very early, as His Lordship had to
leave for London."

"He has. . .gone to London?"

It was almost a cry.

"His Lordship, I understand, had a business en-
gagement. He left a note for Your Ladyship as he was
unable to say good-bye to you."

He brought it on a silver salver and handed it to
Pandia, and she was aware as she took it that her hands
were trembling.

She opened it and saw there were only a few lines.

Then she read:

> *I have left for London early so that I can be*
> *certain of bringing you the book that is important*
> *to both of us. I will see you at tea-time. I know*
> *you understand.*
>
> *J. Stone.*

For a moment it was like a stab from a knife to realise
he had written to her so formally. Then she understood.

It was perhaps his signature which made her aware
that he was thinking of her reputation as the Countess
of Linbourne, and had therefore written in a manner
which nobody could consider indiscreet.

At the same time, he had signed himself with the
name which meant so much to them both in an entirely
different context, showing that he knew she would realise what he dared not write on paper.

She put the note back in the envelope and said:

"His Lordship has to see his Publisher. I had no idea

until I met him yesterday that he was such a famous author!"

"I am surprised you didn't know that, M'Lady," the Butler replied. "Here we're all very proud of the books His Lordship writes, and although His Grace didn't like his being abroad for so many years, he always kept one of His Lordship's books beside his bed."

That was something she too would always do in the future, Pandia thought.

She ate her breakfast hurriedly because she was eager to get to London in good time to be waiting for Lord Silvester when he arrived to see her.

She went up to Lady Anne's bedroom to say goodbye to her, thinking as she did so that the old woman looked very frail, and she had the feeling that she was not likely to live for very much longer.

"I hear the road is quite safe now," Lady Anne said. "It was a very good thing you stayed here last night, and I was delighted to think you were keeping dear Silvester company."

"He is a very interesting person," Pandia replied.

"Yes, and such a kind, thoughtful young man," Lady Anne added. "My brother doted on him, and I think, although of course it is something you must never repeat, that he would have liked Silvester to have been his son and his heir."

"Are his parents dead?" Pandia asked, knowing she was curious and wanting to know everything she could about the man who had come to mean so much to her.

"Actually, his mother died when he was sixteen, and his father married again. His Step-mother did not like Silvester, and as he was unhappy at home he came to us in the holidays. We loved having him."

"But he wanted to travel all over the world," Pandia said, as if she was reasoning it out for herself.

"He was too adventurous not to find the Castle and his home, where his brother was much older than himself, very restricting."

"I can understand that," Pandia said quietly.

She was thinking that Lord Silvester could only be satisfied by reaching far-off horizons, and what he had done physically her father had been forced to do mentally from his small house in Little Barford.

It was something she wanted to talk about to Lord Silvester because he would understand.

Quickly she said good-bye to Lady Anne, and when she was dressed in the smart astrakhan coat with its chinchilla collar, she hurried down to the Hall to find the carriage waiting for her outside.

As she drove away, the horses moving slowly at first over the thickness of the snow which had settled in the drive, she knew that her whole being was pulsating with an irrepressible urgency to reach London and see Lord Silvester.

"I shall see him again. . .I shall talk to him. . .and perhaps he will. . .kiss me!"

She felt herself blush because it seemed immodest to want his kisses. Yet it was impossible to repress the flames which moved in her heart as she thought of last night and the ecstasy he had aroused in her.

'I love him!' Pandia thought. 'I love him with my heart, my soul, and my body, until there is nothing else in the world but him.'

She wondered what he would say if she told him that she was not the Countess of Linbourne but just plain Miss Pandia Hunyadi.

Then she knew that to reveal her real identity to Lord Silvester or to anybody else would be to play Judas to her sister.

Also, she was quite certain that he had no wish to be married.

How could any man who had travelled as he had to strange parts of the world where no white person had been before take a wife with him?

However much he might say he loved her and could never lose her, he was thinking of her as a married woman whose lover he would become, but certainly not as an encumbrance like a wife.

"No," Pandia told herself. "This is just a dream from which neither of us must ever awaken."

At the same time, she knew that for her the dream, if it did not become a nightmare, would be a long misery of loss and growing despair, when she faced the truth that she would never see him again.

She would read his books and hold them next to her heart, but it would not be the same as feeling his lips on hers and, although she blushed at the thought, feeling his hands touching her body.

Once again it flashed through her mind that she had been extremely foolish in not taking what the gods had offered her last night and letting him love her as he wished to do.

At least she would have had that to remember, rather than sending him away saying she had crucified him.

But even as she thought of it she knew that if she had put aside her principles and her ideals, she would have lost something that was very precious.

It was difficult now to realise that, when she had been so shocked at her sister's behaviour, she had not understood the temptation of what Selene had described as "fire in the blood."

Now she did understand, and although what she thought of as her soul told her she had done what was right, her body cried out that now she would never know the meaning of love.

It was the love which had made her mother run away with her father and which had made them blissfully happy in all the years they had been together.

"That is the love I want," Pandia told herself, "but when I held it in my hand I let it go!"

She felt the tears well in her eyes, but she would not let them fall.

All the way to London she sat thinking of Lord Silvester and how much she loved him, and at the same time she felt that her mother was near her.

She felt too she was telling her that she had done

what was right and that eventually, although it was hard to visualise it now, she would cease to regret it.

As the carriage drew up outside the house in Grosvenor Square, the red carpet was rolled down the steps and the Butler stood waiting to welcome her.

"I'm glad to see you, M'Lady," he said. "We were extremely worried last night in case Your Ladyship had started out in the snow and got into difficulties on the road."

"Fortunately, because it was so bad, we never started," Pandia replied, "but remained safe at the Castle."

"That is good news, M'Lady, very good news indeed!" the Butler said.

As she reached the bottom of the stairs, he asked:

"Would Your Ladyship like to have luncheon upstairs in the *Boudoir?*"

"That would be very pleasant," Pandia replied. "I am a little tired after the drive."

She paused. Then she added:

"Lord Silvester Stone will be calling at tea-time."

"Very good, M'Lady. Will you use the Drawing-Room?"

"Yes, please," Pandia answered.

As she went up the stairs she felt a little surge of excitement at the thought of seeing Lord Silvester again, and was certain that the Drawing-Room would be the right background for her as he had thought the Silver Salon was last night.

"I will see him again soon!" she told herself.

Her heart was singing as she hurried towards her bedroom.

* * *

Yvette was waiting for Pandia, and as soon as the door was closed behind her the maid asked:

"Everything all right, *M'mselle?*"

"Everything was marvellous!" Pandia replied. "Except of course, as you know, the snow made it impossible to return last night."

"I worry in case you stranded."

"There were no difficulties," Pandia assured her.

Yvette helped her out of her coat, saying:

"I took out clothes you take home with you."

"It is very good of you," Pandia answered.

At the same time, as she spoke she had a sudden desire to say that as Selene had never thought of her in the past, she had no wish to accept anything from her now.

Then she told herself that if she did that, it would be very foolish, and she was quite certain that she would not be given anything that Selene wanted.

As if she knew what she was thinking, Yvette said:

"*Madame* have many, many gowns no wear. I want give to *les pauvres*—like charity call 'Mrs. Henderson.' "

Pandia laughed. Then as she had a sudden idea she said:

"Has Her Ladyship a riding-habit she does not want? I sometimes have a chance of riding one of the farmers' horses at home, and not only have I grown out of my habit but it is threadbare!"

"I not think of that," Yvette said, "but there are two habits *Madame* say no good."

"Then please may I have them?" Pandia pleaded.

"You leave to me," Yvette replied. "*Aussi* some gowns, *très jolie, très chic! Madame* sometimes wear gown once, twice, then, *voilà,* no more—she no like!"

"That sounds very extravagant!"

Yvette shrugged her shoulders in a typically French gesture.

"*Milor'* verry rich! He like *Madame* by *toujours belle!*"

"Of course she is!" Pandia exclaimed generously, then felt a little embarrassed as if in a way she was complimenting herself.

Yvette started to undo her travelling-gown, saying as she did so:

"Not right, *M'mselle,* you have such poor clothes and stay in country while *Madame* have everything!"

Pandia was wondering how she could answer this when Yvette went on:

"In France everyone in family verry important— *Grandmère, Grandpère, tous les enfants*. Always together verry happy. I miss my family!"

"I am sure you do," Pandia said sympathetically, "just as I miss my father and mother."

"You all alone, *M'mselle?*"

"Except for my old Nanny, who has been with us ever since Her Ladyship and I were born."

"That nice, *M'mselle*. But you *très belle* like *Madame* and you find a man. What you need *un homme et l'amour!*"

The way Yvette spoke told Pandia that that was certainly what *she* wanted, and she said:

"I hope, Yvette, that you will find a man who loves you, and to whom you can be married."

"*Oui, oui, M'mselle!* I save all my money and have large dowry. Easy in France find husband if one have big dowry."

"In which case, if I were in France," Pandia said lightly, "I should have to remain an Old Maid, or, as you say: '*Coiffer Sainte Catherine.*' "

Yvette gave a little cry.

"*Non, non, M'mselle,* not think of bad thing. You be married like *Madame* and have large family."

Pandia thought that was exactly what she wanted but would never have.

Yet, when she went into the flower-scented *Boudoir*, where her luncheon was waiting for her, she thought again that while her sister had everything that was material to make her happy, she did not love the man to whom she was married, nor had she any children.

Then as Pandia ate a delicious meal cooked by an experienced Chef, and served to her by a Butler and two footmen, she could not help thinking that Selene had not only tasted what her father would have described as the "flesh-pots of Egypt" but she had also found love.

True, it was a love that was wrong, a love that would be described as a sin, yet still it was love.

Was it better to love as the gods had loved and found it an irresistible glory, or to be alone without anything except memories?

Pandia did not know the answer, and she wondered if Lord Silvester would be able to give it to her.

Chapter Six

1898

After luncheon Pandia, having changed into one of the prettiest gowns in Selene's wardrobe, found that there was still some time before Lord Silvester would arrive.

She therefore decided to explore the house and found it all very grand and impressive, recognising here and there little bits of her mother's taste which Selene had copied.

There were soft blends of colouring such as her mother had loved and designed for the rooms in their small house in Little Barford.

Selene had done the same but much more grandly and expensively.

Pandia thought it was true that children unconsciously absorbed the environment in which they were brought up, and however much they might wish to escape, it always remained with them fundamentally.

It was the sort of thing she would have liked to talk over with her father, knowing he would have many interesting ideas and be able to give examples from history of what they were discussing.

When she thought of him it was an agony to remember that when she returned to the small house on the edge of the village he would not be there.

"What shall I do with myself?" she wondered.

Then, being afraid to think of the future, she tried

to concentrate on the paintings she saw in the Dining-Room and the books that were in the Earl's Library.

A quick glance told her they were not the sort of books that really interested her.

Most of them were Autobiographies or Biographies of Statesmen, or rather dull-looking reports of speeches that had been made in the House of Lords or in the Parliaments in other parts of the Empire.

However, she thought that if she were married to somebody like the Earl, who was obviously much involved in Government, she would make every effort to understand what interested him so as to be able to talk to him about it.

Then she thought of what she did want to talk about, and found herself glancing every few minutes at the clock, thinking she had never known time to move so slowly.

At last when it was after four she went into the Drawing-Room to wait for Lord Silvester.

It was certainly a room which was a perfect background for Selene and of course herself.

The panelled walls were painted a very soft Nile blue and the cornice was picked out in gold.

There was the inevitable glittering crystal chandelier hanging from the centre of the ceiling and crystal holders for the gas-globes.

They seemed somehow incongruous with the beauty of lighted candles, but as they were new and every fashionable house had been adapted for them, she was aware that Selene could not be behind the fashion.

The furniture was French and of fine quality, and there were many pieces of Sèvres and Dresden china which she knew would have pleased her mother.

The curtains, chairs, and sofas were of a deeper blue than the walls, while all the cushions and the flowers in the room were pink.

She knew that with her white skin and with the glint of red in her hair, she and Selene also would look outstanding against such a background.

She was glad, therefore, that she had chosen a gown that was very simple.

At the same time it made her, she thought a little shyly, look as if she had come down from Olympus.

She thought impatiently that the clock must have stopped; until at last as the big hand reached the half-hour the door opened.

"Lord Silvester Stone, M'Lady!" Bates announced.

As he came into the room it was to Pandia as if a thousand lights lit up in the sky.

He walked towards her, and as he did so she thought she had forgotten how handsome and unusual he looked.

She felt that he came to her like Apollo driving his chariot up the sky to sweep away the darkness of the night, and she could almost see shafts of light coming from him.

She rose to her feet as he entered, and when he was close to her they just stood staring at each other and there was no need for words.

They were speaking in the language of the gods, which was love.

At last when a few seconds, or a century, had passed, Pandia managed to say in a voice that was low and almost incoherent:

"You. . .have come!"

"Did you think I would forget?" Lord Silvester asked.

There was silence. Then he added:

"How can you be a million times more lovely than when I last saw you? It seems utterly impossible that any woman could be so beautiful and still have her feet on the ground!"

Pandia smiled, and it brought a twinkle to his eyes.

"I am sure you are thinking," he said, "that I am being over-emotional and very un-English."

"Actually I was thinking you were being very Greek!" Pandia replied.

They smiled at each other, then Lord Silvester held out the parcel he carried under his arm.

"As I told you I would, I have brought you my book," he said, "as a tribute to lay at your feet."

She took it from him. Then she asked:

"May I open it now?"

"I should be disappointed if you did not do so."

She sat down on the sofa and he sat beside her, watching her as she undid the ribbon with which the book was tied and unwrapped the paper.

It was, as she expected, quite a thin volume.

But she felt as she held it in her hands that it contained all the wisdom she longed for and which she and her father had tried to find.

She saw that the title was *Lights in the Dark*, and she looked at him for an explanation.

"It is very different from my last book," he said as if she had asked the question, "and again quite different from what I am writing now."

"I think this is much deeper," she said. "Am I wrong?"

"No, you are right," he said, "but I expect you cheated and read my thoughts."

"It will be very exciting to read it."

"I hope you will think so," he replied. "I tried to write of all the people who have influenced the thoughts of those who have listened to them—Confucius, Buddha, Socrates, Plato, Aristotle, Christ, Mohammed, and up to modern thinkers such as Darwin."

"It sounds very exciting!"

"I shall be very disappointed if you do not think so. How soon will you be able to read it?"

She looked at him enquiringly, and he said:

"Of course I want you to tell me your opinion of it, including any criticisms, before I leave England."

Pandia looked down at the book in her hand.

She was wondering frantically how she could tell him that after today she would not be able to see him; that she must vanish into the darkness that she was certain he had described most eloquently in his book.

Then as if he could not wait for her answer Lord Silvester asked:

"Have you thought about me?"

"It would be. . .difficult to think of anything. . .else."

"That is what I hoped," he said. "Your face is always before my eyes, and even when you are not there I feel you beside me."

Pandia felt as if he was expressing in his deep voice exactly what she too was feeling, for which she could find no words.

She knew that when she left him she would feel as if he were beside her, and yet it would not be a joy but an agony because he was lost to her forever.

"What I want to ask you is this," Lord Silvester began.

He paused, then he said:

"Look at me! I want to see your eyes! I want them to tell me what you think."

The way he spoke made Pandia quiver. She could feel the sensations he always aroused in her becoming stronger and stronger, and once again the flicker of fire was there.

She knew as the sensations moved within her that she wanted him to kiss her, and she was afraid that when he looked into her eyes he would know exactly what she desired.

Very slowly, although she was frightened, she obeyed him because it was impossible to do anything else.

As she raised her eyes to his, she was spellbound.

She could see the fire blazing within him, and as something wild and wonderful leapt within her, she was drawn to him as if by a magical power that was irresistible.

However much she might argue against it, she knew that just as he wanted her in his arms, that was where she longed to be.

Even as she swayed towards him the door of the Drawing-Room opened.

"His Lordship has returned, M'Lady!"

Bates's voice seemed to break in on what she was feeling as if he spoke from another world in a language which for the moment she did not understand.

Then as Pandia gave an audible gasp, an elderly man, extremely distinguished-looking with a moustache and almost white hair, came into the room.

For a moment she felt as if she was turned to stone and could not move.

Then as he walked briskly down the room towards her, she and Lord Silvester rose to their feet and the Earl asked:

"Are you surprised to see me, my dear? I managed to finish my business and get away early this morning instead of tomorrow!"

He reached Pandia, put out his arms and pulled her towards him, and kissed her cheek.

As if some instinct manipulated her like a puppet, Pandia managed to say in a voice that did not sound like her own:

"I am. . .surprised! Did you have a. . .good journey?"

As she spoke she thought it sounded a very banal remark, but the Earl replied:

"Not too bad! How are you, Silvester? I had no idea you were in this country!"

"It is delightful to see you, Cousin George," Lord Silvester replied, "and I am only, as you might say, 'passing through.'"

"Off again? God knows how you manage to enjoy yourself in all those outlandish places. Poor Dorringcourt was saying the last time I saw him how much he missed you at the Castle."

Without waiting for a reply, the Earl looked at Pandia and said:

"I suppose you met Silvester at the Funeral. I am sure, my dear, you found it very gloomy. I am sorry that I had to ask you to take my place."

"The. . .snow made. . .everything. . .rather difficult," Pandia managed to reply.

As she spoke she realised that the Earl was not listening to her but was looking towards the door where Bates and a footman were bringing in a tray on which were a decanter of whisky and a soda syphon.

"This is what I need," he said in a hearty voice. "It was extremely cold crossing the Channel, and the train was not heated as well as it might have been. I intend to write to the Chairman of the Southern Railway and tell him so!"

Bates poured out a whisky and soda for the Earl, and another footman brought in a tea-table with the same elaborate amount of silver and profusion of delicacies as had been served at the Castle.

"Will you join me in a drink, Silvester?" the Earl asked as if he had suddenly thought of it. "Or would you prefer partaking of what I always think of as a woman's meal?"

"I think on this occasion I would prefer a cup of tea," Lord Silvester answered. "Then I must be going."

With difficulty Pandia bit back the cry that came to her lips.

She could see by the expression in his eyes that he disliked seeing her with the man he thought of as her husband and was finding, as she was, that the spell that had joined them together had been roughly broken.

'The only fortunate thing,' Pandia thought, 'is that the Earl seems to have no idea I am not Selene.'

He had now seated himself on the other side of the fireplace and was saying briskly:

"The weather in Paris was far better than here, and I can say without conceit that mine was a very successful visit!"

Because Lord Silvester did not say anything, Pandia replied:

"I am so glad it was. . .successful and you. . .managed to do whatever was expected of you so. . .quickly."

"The Prime Minister will be delighted at what I have achieved," the Earl said in a tone of satisfaction, "and now I shall have a chance of telling him about it tomorrow morning before he goes to the country for the weekend."

"Yes. . .of course," Pandia murmured.

"How is your brother," the Earl asked Lord Silvester, "still in Egypt?"

Automatically while the Earl was talking Pandia had poured out a cup of tea for Lord Silvester, but now without touching it he rose to his feet.

"As I have a great deal to do before I leave at the end of next week," he said, "I am sure you will forgive me if I hurry to my next appointment."

"I am glad you were able to be at the Funeral, Silvester," the Earl replied. "Come and see us when next you visit England. Will that be in five years, or ten?"

He laughed, but it did not seem like a joke to Pandia.

She only felt as if this was the end of everything that mattered to her.

It was as if for one moment she had held the blue-bird of happiness in her hands, and now it was flying away into the sky and in a few seconds it would be lost to her forever.

"As you are well aware," Lord Silvester replied to the Earl, "when one is travelling in far-off places, time ceases to exist. A reluctant mule or a leaking dhow may make the difference of a month or a year in one's plans, and there is nothing one can do about it."

"Better you than me!" the Earl retorted. "Even if our railway-carriages are inadequately heated, they get there on time."

Lord Silvester held out his hand to Pandia.

As she put hers into it she had an almost uncontrollable impulse to hold on to him, to beg him to stay or to take her with him—anything he wished, but not to leave her.

Then as she felt his vibrations so strongly that it was almost as if they hurt her, he released her hand and turned to the Earl.

"Good-bye, Cousin George," he said. "Do not move. I forgot to tell you how much Cousin Anne missed you yesterday. She is growing very frail and I do not think she will live very long."

"That is what they were saying the last time I saw her," the Earl replied, "but all our relatives, Silvester, cling tenaciously to life, and she may easily live as long as poor Rudolph did, if not longer."

Lord Silvester walked towards the door.

Feeling that it was impossible to move, Pandia stood where he had left her, watching him go.

As he turned the handle he looked back. Their eyes met and she felt as if they touched each other across eternity.

Then he was gone.

"Nice fellow, Silvester," the Earl remarked, "but like so many young people today, always on the move, never ready to settle down and live a decent life."

"He. . .writes very. . .successful books," Pandia managed to say, as if she felt she must stand up for him.

"And I hear they make money," the Earl remarked, "although Silvester does not need it. But between ourselves, I cannot understand a word he writes!"

He laughed before he added:

"It takes me all my time to live in the world today, without anybody rambling on about what happened in the past!"

Pandia did not answer. She was sipping her tea as if she hoped the warmth of it would somehow take away the feeling of isolation that was like an icicle round her heart.

The Earl finished his glass of whisky.

"I am going to the Study," he said. "I have a number of letters I have to write before dinner, and I will tell you then all about Paris."

"That will be very . . . interesting," Pandia managed to reply.

The Earl rose from his chair, walked across the room, and went out without looking back.

Only when she was alone did Pandia draw in her breath and realise how tense she had been with fear that the Earl would realise she was not his wife.

However, miraculously he had accepted her without question.

She thought she must find Yvette and ask her what she should do.

She picked up the book which Lord Silvester had left between them on the sofa and ran across the room as if somehow she must escape from her own fears.

Only as she stepped into the Hall did she with a superhuman effort manage to walk with dignity, aware that the two footmen in attendance would think it strange if she tore past them as she wanted to do.

When she reached her bedroom she was not surprised to find that Yvette was there waiting for her.

As she entered the room she shut the door behind her and resisted an impulse to lock it.

"His Lordship. . .is back!" she managed to gasp in a voice that did not sound like her own.

"Oui, M'mselle," Yvette replied. *"C'est incroyable! Milor'* not guess you not *Madame?"*

"No, he was not in the least suspicious," Pandia replied in a whisper, "but I am frightened. . .very frightened, Yvette. Can we not reach Her Ladyship and tell her she must return at once?"

"Impossible, M'mselle!" Yvette replied. *"Madame* certain *Monsieur* not return 'til tomorrow. She not in London!"

"N-not in. . .London?" Pandia exclaimed. "Do you mean that you. . .cannot arrange for her to. . .return tonight?"

"Non, M'mselle."

Then as Yvette saw how pale Pandia had gone and the fear that was in her eyes, she said quickly:

"Not worry, *M'mselle! Milor'* sleeps in own bedroom, and he tired after journey. Paris a long way an' *Monsieur* not a young man."

Pandia felt herself relax a little. At the same time, she was still afraid.

It was one thing to impersonate her twin sister at a

Funeral, but quite another to play the part of wife to her husband.

She moved farther into the room, and Yvette said:

"Lie down, *M'mselle*. You have shock! Rest 'til dinner, you feel better."

Because there was nothing else she could do, Pandia let Yvette take off her gown which she had chosen so carefully for Lord Silvester, and put on her nightgown.

She got into bed, and when Yvette had tidied the room and lowered the lights, she left Pandia alone.

"I wake you seven o'clock, *M'mselle*," she said. "Not worry. Everything all right. *Madame* return tomorrow morning."

The way she spoke sounded reassuring, but when she was alone Pandia felt she was still tense with fear.

Now in retrospect the awful moment when the Earl had come into the Drawing-Room made her feel as if she had stood on the very edge of a precipice and nothing could save her from falling over.

However, he had not realised that she was not Selene. But why should he when they were so alike and he had no idea even of her existence?

She was indeed convinced that if she was married to a man and the situation was reversed, the instant he touched her he would know that Selene was not his wife.

But the Earl was not the man of her dreams, and all that mattered now was that she must be clever enough to continue to impersonate Selene until she returned.

She felt, now that she had met the Earl, that distinguished as he might be, he was much too old a husband for her sister.

At the same time, he was a man, and she was sure he was proud and would be extremely jealous if he thought his wife was being unfaithful to him.

He would be ruthless, perhaps cruel, in defence of his honour.

Pandia's instinct, which invariably told her the truth about people, convinced her that the Earl was the type of man who would never forgive his wife for humiliating him.

'I must protect Selene, I must save her, whatever happens to me,' Pandia thought.

Because she was so frightened, she prayed frantically that the Earl would continue to accept her as his wife and that it would never cross his mind that she could be anything else.

Pandia lay thinking of the predicament she was in and, when she did think of herself, of how she had lost Lord Silvester.

She had known that after tomorrow she would never see him again.

But somehow she had been sure that they would have been able to take leave of each other in a way which would leave them both with a memory of happiness which nothing could destroy.

Instead he had left her abruptly, and all that she had to comfort her was the book he had given her.

She had put it down on the bed beside her, and now, almost as if she was afraid to do so in case she was disappointed, she opened it.

It was then that she saw the inscription inside, which read:

> *I searched the world, the sky, the sea,*
> *The mountain peaks and tried to find*
> *The Light that other men have tried*
> *To see.*
> *Alone I climbed, alone I sought*　＼
> *The moonlight which a goddess brought*
> *To me.*

He had not signed it, but she knew he had written it for her, and while anybody else reading it would not understand, she did.

For a moment Pandia felt as if his arms were round her and his lips were on hers.

Then as she turned to the next page, the print blurred

in front of her eyes, and her tears made it impossible to read.

He had gone out of her life as swiftly as he had come into it, and she would never see him again.

Even if he tried, and she thought it unlikely, to see her by calling again when he thought the Earl would not be there, she would not be aware of it.

"I must warn Selene that we met at the Funeral," she told herself.

But tears, slow and painful, as if each one were a drop of blood, were pouring down her face.

Her whole body was yearning for the man she loved with an inexpressible agony that she had never felt before.

She pushed the book away from her and, turning over, buried her face in her pillow.

*   *   *

"Paris was really quite enjoyable," the Earl was saying at dinner, as the servants offered them dish after dish of superbly prepared food.

"I was thinking," he went on, "that I must take you there next time I go. The Ambassador is eager to give a special dinner-party for us at the Embassy, and a number of distinguished Statesmen have said how much they would like to meet you!"

The Earl smiled as he helped himself to another ortolan and said:

"The Prince of Wales is such a success in Paris, not only with French Society, which he found somewhat dull, but with the Demi-Mondaines and the actresses who were all asking when he will be joining them again."

"Did you have time to go to the Theatre or the Opera?" Pandia asked.

She had been trying to remember everything she had heard about Paris.

Actually, to dine with the Earl was very much easier

than she had expected, for the simple reason that he
liked to talk and all she really had to do was to listen.

"Not on this visit," he replied, "because it was too
short."

He then went into a long description of the times he
had been in Paris before their marriage and the gaieties
to which his French friends had taken him.

If she had not been so nervous, Pandia thought, she
would have enjoyed hearing about what was yet another world of which she was completely ignorant.

The Earl's stories of the leading actresses in Paris,
whom he described as being covered with ospreys and
pearls, and the extravagance of the parties that were
given for them, made Pandia listen wide-eyed.

"I suppose I should not be telling you this, my dear,"
he said, "but men make fools of themselves over these
women."

"Are they very beautiful?" Pandia asked.

The Earl chuckled.

"Not compared to you, but they have a gamin attrac-
tiveness which is very French, and undoubtedly very
alluring."

He sounded almost as if he were enjoying a mouthful
of *pâté de foie gras*. Pandia wondered if Lord Silvester
admired women like that and if there were alluring
women not only in Paris but in all the countries he
visited.

She had read that Arab women were alluring, especially the dancers, and she felt a sudden knife-like pain
which she knew was one of jealousy.

Because she was suddenly aware that the Earl had
said something to which she had not replied, she said
quickly:

"Do tell me more! I find it fascinating!"

"I am surprised!" he remarked.

"Why?"

"You are usually not very interested in what I have to
tell you."

"That is not true," Pandia said quickly, "but sometimes I have a lot I want to tell you."

"You have not told me," he replied, "what happened at the Funeral, not that I suspect it was anything but exceedingly gloomy, and I am sure the Castle was cold and even more draughty than usual!"

"Let us talk about more cheerful things," Pandia said. "Tell me more about Paris and the party you attended last night."

It was a bold venture because he had not actually said he had gone to a party, and she thought he hesitated before he replied:

"I am not certain it is something I should tell you, but after dinner was over, I and a few friends went off, as you might say, 'on the town.'"

"Where did you go? And are the places you visit in Paris very different from those in London?"

Because she encouraged him and he was also enjoying his dinner and the wine he was drinking, the Earl became very eloquent.

She was sure that like most old men he wanted to talk and have an appreciative audience to encourage him.

In fact, they sat for so long over dinner that Pandia was sure that the servants were waiting impatiently for them to retire to the Drawing-Room.

She did suggest that she should leave him to his port, but the Earl said:

"No, you stay, my dear. It is not often we are alone, and I am quite sure without looking at my engagement-book that either we are giving a dinner-party here tomorrow night or we have to go out to one."

Because Pandia had not the slightest idea of what they were doing, she did not reply, and he went on:

"I have often thought that I see far too little of you, but I suppose that is the penalty of success! You, because you are so beautiful, and as for me, when the Prince of Wales does not want me, the Prime Minister does!"

"I am sure you are a. . .great help to them both," Pandia managed to say.

"Where the Prince is concerned, I manage to amuse him," the Earl replied, "and he finds me useful because I have made him quite a lot of money in the last six months."

Pandia looked at him questioningly, and he said as if she had asked the question:

"I am not pretending that I know everything, like the Rothschilds and Cassel, when it comes to investments, but I am delighted to say my tips have 'turned up trumps'!"

Pandia remembered having heard that the Prince was always in debt and had often needed helping out of difficulty by his friends.

She had somehow not expected Selene's husband to be rich enough to be a leading figure in the Financial World, and she said:

"You must be very clever to do better than the wealthy gentlemen you have just mentioned."

"I am glad you appreciate the fact," the Earl said a little drily, "and that reminds me, Selene, I thought the Prince was being far too attentive towards you the last time we dined at Marlborough House."

His voice sharpened as he said:

"I know his reputation where beautiful women are concerned! So let me make it quite clear that if I have the slightest suspicion that he is being too familiar, I shall take you to the country and leave you there!"

The way he spoke made Pandia draw in her breath. Then with an effort she managed to exclaim:

"How can you think such things! His Royal Highness is not really interested in me! After all, he has other. . . ladies."

Again she was speaking without much knowledge of what she was saying, but apparently it was the right thing, for the Earl answered:

"That is true! But as you well know, I am very jealous

where you are concerned, and I am not having anybody 'poaching on my preserves'!"

Pandia thought as he spoke that the Earl would be furious if he had the slightest idea of what her sister was actually doing, and would punish her in a manner which she could not bear to think about.

For Selene to be incarcerated in the country or ostracised by the Social World would be a punishment tantamount to being sent to the gallows.

She knew that she must warn her sister that the way she was behaving might prove disastrous.

The Earl pushed back his chair.

"We might as well go into the Drawing-Room," he said, "and I expect you are tired, so we had better go to bed early, especially as I have a long day ahead of me tomorrow."

"A. . .long day?" Pandia questioned.

"I told you before I left for Paris that I would have to be back early to see the Prime Minister," he replied, "and there is a Reception of some sort in the afternoon, but I have forgotten what it is."

"Oh, yes. . .of course," Pandia agreed.

She hoped he would not question her, and fortunately as they walked towards the Drawing-Room he began to talk about something else.

"I think the Fragonard has been returned from being cleaned," he said. "Are you pleased with it? You always told me it was one of your favourite paintings."

"I am delighted!" Pandia exclaimed. "It certainly looks very much better than it did before."

She had no idea what painting he was referring to, and because she thought he might question her further, she said:

"Did you see any paintings you thought of buying while you were in Paris?"

The Earl was immediately diverted.

"Not this time," he said, "but everybody was laughing about a new group of painters which are even greater charlatans than the original 'Impressionists.'

Personally, I would not give sixpence for any of their work!"

"What do they look like?" Pandia asked.

Now the Earl was off on one of his pet subjects: the crime that was called "Modern Art" and was the work of lunatics and drug-addicts.

Pandia then diverted him to carry on from there to the paintings he did like and which he would wish to own and add to the large collection he already had in the country.

Glancing at the clock on the mantelpiece without appearing to do so, she realised it was nearly eleven, and she heaved a little sigh of relief.

"You suggested we should go to bed early," she said, "and now, because you have been so interesting, it is growing quite late."

"I suppose you want your 'beauty sleep,'" he remarked, "and I admit to being tired myself. At the same time, I have enjoyed being with you tonight, my dear, more than I have for a long time."

Pandia had the sudden feeling that he was going to put his arm round her waist, and she moved swiftly towards the door.

She pulled it open as the Earl followed her and they stepped into the Hall where the night footman was standing by the front door.

They walked together slowly up the stairs because Pandia knew that after such a large dinner the Earl would have no wish to hurry.

Only as they turned along the corridor towards their bedrooms did he put his arm through hers and say:

"I suppose I have been rather remiss in not telling you that you are looking very lovely! I like you in that gown."

"I am glad," Pandia said.

He stopped before they reached her bedroom door.

"Shall I come and say good-night to you tonight?"

There was a note of passion in the Earl's voice, and Pandia said quickly:

"I. . .I am very tired after a really horrible journey back through the snow. . .and I also have a headache."

She knew without his saying so that he was disappointed, and as he followed her into her bedroom, her heart was beating frantically and she felt her lips were dry.

But to her relief Yvette was there, and as if her French sense told her what was happening, she curtseyed to the Earl and said:

"*Bonsoir, Milor'*, I glad *Monsieur* return safely. I know long journey to *Parie* and verry unpleasant in winter."

"Nevertheless, I expect you are sometimes homesick for your native land!" the Earl replied genially.

"*C'est vrai, Milor'*, but I happy to look after *Madame*. She find yesterday *très désagréable* in snow. *Je suis effraye* she catch cold."

"You did not tell me that!" the Earl said, turning to Pandia.

"It is. . .not bad," she replied. "Only a rather sore throat."

"I hot drink for *Madame*," Yvette went on, "but she not give cold to *Milor'* with many, many speeches to make."

"That is true, Yvette," the Earl agreed. "A cold in the nose is very inhibiting when one is speaking."

He went to Pandia and put his arm round her.

"Good-night, my dear. Sleep well."

He kissed her quickly on the cheek, then went from the room, closing the door behind him.

They waited until they had heard him going into his own room. Then Pandia said:

"Thank you, Yvette! You said exactly the right thing!"

The maid undid her gown at the back, and because she still felt frightened and had nobody else in whom to confide, Pandia said frantically:

"Supposing. . .just supposing, Yvette, he comes to say. . .good-night to me as he. . .suggested?"

"He no come, *M'mselle*," Yvette said, "but if *Milor'*

peep in and you asleep, fast asleep, *impossible* wake you."

"And if he does?"

"You beg *Monsieur*, 'cause you love him, go away."

Yvette threw out her arms in a gesture that was very French and laughed.

"*Très stupide*. We think of this before. *M'mselle* sneeze at dinner. *Un peu de poivre*, an' also you be hoarse, *M'mselle*."

"It is too late now," Pandia said, "and I suppose it would be wrong to. . .lock the door?"

Yvette gave a scream.

"*C'est folie, M'mselle*, an insult! *Milor'* suspicious *immédiatement* you interested 'nother man!"

"He has said that he is. . .jealous," Pandia murmured.

"*Très* jealous! *Madame* so beautiful. Any man afraid of thieves when he possess such treasure."

Pandia wanted to laugh at the way Yvette spoke.

Then she remembered that as far as Selene was concerned, a thief had already stolen the Earl's "treasure" from him, although he was not aware of it.

She suddenly thought the whole thing was sordid and degrading and, as far as she was concerned, humiliating.

She knew how horrified her mother would have been if she knew that at this moment she was desperately nervous in case Selene's husband should approach her, and it would be disastrous if she told him the truth.

"Not frightened, *M'mselle*," Yvette said. "*Milor' toujours* verry careful he not risk cold, too busy in the House of *Milor's*."

"I. . .I hope you are right," Pandia said nervously.

At the same time, as she got into bed, she knew she would lie awake, afraid of every creak of the floorboards, and knowing that if the door opened she would be so terrified that her heart might stop beating.

Chapter Seven

Pandia did not fall asleep until it was nearly dawn and then awoke because Yvette came into the room to pull back the curtains.

She felt sleepy and heavy-eyed until she remembered that the Earl was in the house, then was suddenly wide awake.

A young housemaid had come in with Yvette and was now lighting the fire.

It was a luxury that Pandia had enjoyed the first night of her arrival and also at the Castle.

Her mother had told her that in grand houses where there were a lot of servants, the first thing that happened in the morning was that maids lit fires in all the ladies' rooms.

Pandia wished now that she could tell her mother it was happening in hers and how luxurious it made her feel.

Then she could think of nothing but that Selene would be back soon and she must remember all the things she had to tell her.

Yvette did not speak to her until the housemaid, having now got the fire burning brightly, withdrew. Then she said:

"You not wish, *M'mselle*, breakfast downstairs, so I breeng to you."

Pandia gave a little sigh of relief.

During the night she had wondered what she should

say to the Earl at breakfast and whether she should pretend that her cold was worse or better.

Then she thought that as Selene was returning today, she might be annoyed to have a cold "thrust upon her," as it were.

Yvette went to the door, where a footman was waiting outside with her breakfast on a tray, and brought it in and set it down on a table beside the bed.

Pandia thought it was the last time she would have anything so elegant as a silver covered dish and what she recognised as a Crown Derby cup and plates.

There were also a small silver Queen Anne teapot, a milk jug, and a sugar basin.

"Eat, *M'mselle!*" Yvette admonished her. "Nothing better when worried."

Pandia smiled, knowing this was true.

Then she asked in a whisper:

"What time do you think Her Ladyship will return?"

"Early, *M'mselle*. Big luncheon *pour Madame aujourd'-hui.*"

This was what the Earl had said last night, Pandia thought with relief.

At the same time, she knew this might be the last time that she would see her sister, and it hurt her to think that, having done what was wanted or required of her, she was so easily dispensable.

She had finished her breakfast and Yvette was taking the tray away when the door opened and the Earl came into her bedroom.

He looked very distinguished in the clothes he was wearing for his appointment with the Prime Minister.

As he reached her Pandia was very conscious of her hair falling over her shoulders and that she was sitting up in bed in a nightgown.

"Good-morning, my dear," the Earl said. "I hope you are feeling better?"

"Much better, thank you," Pandia replied. "Yvette made me a warm drink, and I do not think I will have a cold after all."

As she spoke, she thought that she had cleared the way for Selene.

Then she wondered if she had been somewhat indiscreet.

Yvette had left the room, and the Earl sat down on the side of the bed as Lord Silvester had done and Pandia saw an expression in his eyes which made her feel frightened.

"You are very beautiful this morning!" he said. "I was thinking last night that we must make arrangements to be more often alone than we have been just recently. I shall not go to the Club this afternoon, as I had planned, but shall come back here, and I think, my dearest, we might have a very happy time before we have to dine at the Foreign Office."

There was no mistaking his meaning, and despite the fact that he thought he was speaking to her sister, Pandia felt the colour rising in her cheeks.

"I only wish I could stay longer at this moment," the Earl said.

Now there was a definite note of passion in his voice that she could not mistake.

He gave a little laugh and added:

"Damn Prime Ministers, and all those who come between a man and his wife!"

He bent forward as he spoke, and would have kissed Pandia on the mouth if she had not turned her head at the very last moment so that his lips rested on her cheek.

"Be. . .careful!" she said hurriedly. "I might. . .still be. . .infectious!"

She felt the Earl's lips and moustache against her cheek as she spoke.

Then as he raised his head he said:

"I am not afraid, and I will hurry back this evening! Take care of your self, my beautiful wife!"

He rose from the bed as he spoke, and when he reached the door he looked back and Pandia knew that he was definitely excited by her.

Then, almost as if he forced himself to do his duty, he went from the bedroom, shutting the door behind him.

She gave a little gasp and lay back against the pillows, thinking that once again she had stood on the edge of a ravine and had somehow avoided falling into it.

It flashed through her mind that if the Earl had not had an early morning appointment with the Prime Minister, she might have been in a very different position and one from which it would have been extremely hard to extricate herself.

But she was safe—safe until Selene returned—although her heart was still thumping and she knew how frightened she had been.

Yvette came back into the room.

"*Milor'* left," she said. "I get bath, *M'mselle*, you dress before *Madame* return."

Pandia did not answer.

She felt she could not tell Yvette, however confidential Selene might be with her, what the Earl had said or what he was planning.

She knew that her mother would have been shocked by Selene's taking a servant into her confidence when it concerned her relationship with her husband—and her lover.

Pandia too believed that intimate matters should be kept to oneself, and she would have to tell Selene privately what had happened and what the Earl intended.

She lay back on her pillows, feeling her agitation gradually subside until once again she was thinking of Lord Silvester.

If only she could see him, she thought, to say goodbye and to talk to him about his book.

She had kept it beside her bed, but she did not wish to open it until she could appreciate what he had written without feeling agitated about anything else.

Once she was home, there would be nothing to upset her today or tomorrow, this year or next year.

But she did not want to think about that!

Instead it was an agonising feeling to know that she and Lord Silvester were only a few streets apart, but already, because she was leaving, it was as if he were on the other side of the world.

Yvette came in to say that her bath was ready, and when Pandia had enjoyed the warm, scented water she dressed herself in the plain, serviceable under-clothes she had worn when she arrived.

Then she put on her own cheap black gown that she had bought for her father's Funeral.

After the lovely gowns she had worn belonging to Selene, she felt it was even duller and cheaper than it had been when she first arrived.

Yvette arranged her hair again in the same way as Selene's because she thought it might be dangerous to go back to being herself before she reached home.

"You do like this, *M'mselle*," she said. "An' look *très jolie*. When you wear *Madame*'s gowns I pack, *tout le monde* admire you."

Pandia smiled, but she thought there was no point in saying that "everybody" would consist only of Nanny and the people in the village.

She doubted if the Vicar or the Doctor would notice what she was wearing, and her only audience would be herself looking at her reflection in the mirror and thinking she saw Selene.

"I find two riding-'abits," Yvette was saying, "two smart 'ats, gloves, boots!"

"That is wonderful!" Pandia exclaimed. "I am so very, very grateful. I want to give you a little present, Yvette. I am afraid it is not very much, but I came away in such a hurry. When I get home I will send you some more money."

"*Non, non, M'mselle!*" Yvette cried. "You keep! You verry poor."

"Not so poor that I cannot show my gratitude for all your kindness to me," Pandia replied. "I would have been very frightened if you had not been here, and it will be very exciting to have some lovely clothes to wear."

She took two sovereigns, which was all she had with her, from her hand-bag and put them into Yvette's hand.

The maid would have refused it, but Pandia said:

"For your dowry, Yvette, and I shall pray that you will find somebody kind, handsome, and rich whom you will love and who will love you."

Yvette laughed. Then she said:

"*Merci, M'mselle*, an' I pray for you *toujours*, and St. Jude answer my prayers."

Pandia thought that in her case St. Jude would fail, but she said again:

"I will pray very hard for you, Yvette."

She knew that the maid was touched by her sincerity, and she was just about to ask Yvette what was in the trunks when there was a knock on the door.

Yvette gave her a meaningful glance and walked across the room to open it.

"Mrs. Henderson's here to see Her Ladyship," Pandia heard the footman say.

"Lady for the clothes!" Yvette exclaimed. "Ask her come up, an' carry trunks downstairs."

"Very good, Miss Yvette."

Yvette waited by the door, and neither she nor Pandia spoke until two minutes later, when Selene, with the black crêpe veil over her face, came into the room.

As Yvette shut the door behind her she flung back her veil, saying:

"Has His Lordship come back? I thought I saw his travelling-cloak in the Hall."

Before Yvette could answer, Pandia, who had risen to her feet, said:

"He came back yesterday at tea-time!"

"Why on earth should he have done that?" Selene asked.

She was pulling off the widow's bonnet as she spoke, and Yvette took Pandia's cloak from her shoulders.

Underneath she was wearing a very elegant gown that accentuated the curves of her figure and made her skin seem dazzlingly white.

There was, however, an angry expression on her face as she said:

"How could I have imagined that he would come back sooner than he said he would? I hope he had no suspicions about you?"

"None at all!" Pandia replied.

Although she did not say so, she knew her sister was relieved.

Then, as if she must vent her anger on somebody, she said sharply:

"Come along, Pandia! Do hurry up and go! There is no point in hanging about!"

"I. . .I have a lot to. . .tell you."

"There is no time to talk," Selene said sharply. "The same carriage that brought you here will take you home, but do not allow the men to speak to Nanny. You must tell them to hurry back as quickly as they can, Yvette."

"I tell Mr. Bates," Yvette replied. "I say urgent."

She carried the bonnet that Selene had discarded to Pandia, who said as she took it from her:

"Selene, I must speak to you! I have to tell you whom I met at the Funeral, and what. . .your husband said to me."

"I am not in the slightest bit interested in the Funeral now that it is over," Selene said, "and I am quite able to manage George!"

Pandia wanted to argue, but Selene added in an even sharper voice than she had used before:

"Do hurry, Pandia! I cannot think why you are dawdling about when you are well aware that it is dangerous for us to be together!"

She must have realised as she spoke that Pandia was hurt by her tone, for she said in a different voice:

"I am grateful to you, of course I am grateful, but this is not the moment for us to talk, and you must be aware

that the sooner you go back to Little Barford, the safer
it will be."

She paused before she asked:

"You are quite certain nobody suspected you were
not me?"

"Nobody!" Pandia replied. "But. . ."

She was going to say that Lord Silvester might call
and that if he did he would talk of his book, but before
she could do so, her sister said:

"That is splendid! Good-bye, dearest! If I ever want
you again, I know you will not fail me."

She kissed Pandia's cheek, then walked away and
went into the bathroom.

For a moment Pandia could hardly believe that she
had left her.

Then as Yvette fastened her cape in the front and
pulled her veil over her face, she was aware that it was
the end.

She picked up her own gloves and the worn hand-
bag, and Yvette, as if she must obey her mistress,
opened the bedroom door for her.

Only as Pandia passed her did she say softly:

"*Bonne chance, M'mselle!* I pray!"

"Thank you, Yvette."

Then she was walking down the passage and down
the stairs to the Hall.

Because Mrs. Henderson was obviously of no importance, the Butler was not there to see her off, only
the footman, and there was no red carpet on the steps
outside.

She got into the carriage and realised as she did so
that there were three trunks on top of it, and when
they drove off she saw there were two large hat-boxes
on the small seat opposite her inside the carriage.

She thought that Yvette had been very kind to give
her so much, but she wished that it had been Selene
who had taken so much trouble.

Then she told herself that whatever Selene felt for
her, she would always love her twin sister and be very

grateful for an experience that might never come again in her life and which she would never forget.

Even so, on the way home to Little Barford, as she thought of Lord Silvester her heart was aching.

Although she would always be inexpressibly grateful to have met him, she would never again be able to dream that one day she would find a man whom she would love and who would love her.

She had found him not in her dreams but in reality, and she had lost him, also in reality.

"I love him. . .and I shall love him all my life," Pandia whispered as she fought against her tears.

*　　*　　*

Because it had not snowed during the night, the roads were practically clear and the horses reached Little Barford without any delays.

As they drove up to the house at the end of the village, Pandia felt a sudden warmth inside her because she had come home.

She had gone adventuring, but now it was all over, and even though her father was not there, there would be Nanny and everything that was familiar and safe.

The footman opened the carriage-door, and as she expected the front door of the house was unbolted, and as she went into the Hall, Nanny appeared from the kitchen.

"You're back, dearie!" she exclaimed. "I've been worrying about you and half-afraid I'd never see you again!"

Pandia kissed her through the veil.

"I am back, quite safe and sound!" she said. "And, please, have you any money? I need a sovereign for the coachman."

She thought Nanny was going to argue that it was too much, but instead she went into the kitchen and brought back a number of silver coins, which Pandia thought must be the last of the housekeeping money.

While she was doing so, the footman was carrying in her trunks one after another, then the hat-boxes.

Pandia thanked him and said as she did so:

"I am sorry to be inhospitable and not offer you both a cup of tea, but Her Ladyship was very anxious that you should return immediately."

"That's all right, Ma'am."

He touched his cockaded hat and went out through the front door, closing it behind him.

Pandia waited until she heard the wheels of the carriage driving away, then she pulled off the widow's bonnet and was glad to be free of the constraining veil.

"Well, Miss Selene's certainly been generous!" Nanny said, looking at the trunks. "Not that it's not about time! What's she given you?"

"I have not seen them," Pandia answered. "Her maid packed them for me and they were all things that Selene no longer wanted."

Nanny sniffed but she only said:

"We're going to find it difficult to get them heavy trunks upstairs. It'll be better to unpack them down here."

"Of course!" Pandia agreed. "That is a sensible idea! They are much too heavy for you to move about."

"First you're going to have something to eat," Nanny said. "Luncheon's ready. Are you going to eat with me as you usually do, or have you grown too grand?"

"I am going to eat with you, Nanny, and I have so much to tell you."

She followed Nanny into the kitchen and sat down at the table, saying:

"First I must tell you about Selene's house in London, which is very large and beautifully decorated and just what Mama would like. Then I will tell you all about the Castle."

"The Castle?" Nanny asked. "What were you doing in a Castle?"

It was then that Pandia remembered that Nanny did not know why Selene had wanted her to go to London.

She was well aware that Nanny had not missed the fact that she had been disguised as a widow, and because she was quick-witted she would undoubtedly guess why she had a veil over her face.

Then she thought the safest and wisest thing to do would be to tell Nanny the truth: that Selene had wanted her to take her place at the Funeral.

But loyalty prevented her from telling Nanny the reason why. She therefore explained that Selene had no wish to waste her time attending a Funeral of an old relation whom she had never even met.

In fact, as she had promised to go to a very glamorous and exciting party, she had asked Pandia to take her place.

Pandia thought as she was telling her the story that Nanny seemed to believe it, but she was not completely certain.

Nanny knew them both so well, and although she had adored Selene when she was young, she had been just as hurt as Pandia had when she left home after her mother's death.

Because it was so like a fairy-story, Pandia told Nanny about the magnificence of the Castle and also described in detail Selene's house in London and how important her husband was.

"He must have thought it strange that he hadn't met you before, Miss Pandia!" Nanny remarked.

"I expect Selene had a good explanation as to why I could not go to London," Pandia replied lightly.

"Did you find Miss Selene happy?" Nanny asked.

Pandia had the idea that she was probing a little too deeply, and she said quickly:

"The Earl adores her! Now, let us go and look in the trunks. I admit to being very curious!"

* * *

The next day it seemed to Pandia that she and Nanny spent all their time unpacking.

Never had she dreamt that she would ever possess such lovely things as those Yvette had packed for her.

There were not only the habits she had longed for

and which looked to her so perfect that she could not
understand why Selene wished to get rid of them.

There were also gowns of every description, including a large number of summer-gowns which Selene
must have discarded just so that she could have new
ones next year.

Nanny insisted on leaving those in the trunk.

"You've nowhere to put them, Miss Pandia," she said
firmly, "and they'll not hurt, seeing as how they're
packed with so much tissue-paper!"

Pandia saw the wisdom of this even though she would
have liked to keep looking at them.

But already the wardrobe in her own bedroom was
full and so were the ones in her mother's room.

She made another small bedroom upstairs into a
wardrobe-room and there were gowns on the bed and
even hanging on picture-hooks on the walls.

The evening-gowns were lovely, but Pandia said as
they took them out one by one:

"I wonder what the villagers would think if they saw
me in one of these."

"They'd decide you were mad," Nanny said sharply,
"and the Vicar would undoubtedly think you were a
'Scarlet Woman'!"

They both laughed because they knew that the Vicar,
who was a bachelor, was noted as being very Puritanical
in his attitude towards the women worshippers in the
village who, as Nanny always said, "made eyes at him."

The hat-boxes contained not only a top-hat and a
bowler to wear with the habits but also a number of
very pretty other hats.

There were in addition several feather-trimmed bon-
nets in which it was fashionable to travel and which
could be worn with cloaks or coats which had fur collars.

What delighted Pandia perhaps more than anything
else was that Yvette had included some of the lovely
under-clothes which she had worn with Selene's gowns.

There were nightgowns so diaphanous that Nanny

said sharply she would "catch her death of cold" in them.

There were lace-trimmed chemises and petticoats that appeared to be in perfect condition.

"Extravagant! That's what Miss Selene's become!" Nanny said sharply. "Why does she want to get rid of these things when she couldn't have worn them more than half-a-dozen times?"

"I expect they bored her," Pandia replied, "and personally, Nanny, I am very thankful to have them."

"As I said before," Nanny answered sharply, as if she must have the last word, "it's better late than never, and let us hope that this sort of turn-out is the first of many."

She marched up the stairs as she spoke, carrying an armful of silk and lace-trimmed under-clothes.

Pandia sat on the floor of the Hall and thought that one blessing was that she would not have to buy any more clothes for a very long time.

The next day, which was Sunday, she went to Church, and every time she knelt to pray she felt as if Lord Silvester were beside her and she could feel his vibrations as she had done when they had knelt side by side at the Funeral.

Then because she loved him she prayed that he would be safe on his journey to Morocco and that sometimes he would think of her as she would be thinking continually of him.

Her one joy was to read his book.

As she had expected, it was fascinating. Every word had a special meaning for her and somehow enriched her mind and broadened her horizons, just as his other books had done.

Then she told herself resolutely that it was time she went back to work on her father's book, and if it was to be finished she must waste no more time in thinking about Lord Silvester.

She remembered how much she owed to her father and how much he would have liked his last work to be published, even though there were very few people who would be interested in reading it.

After breakfast she said to Nanny:

"I am going to work on Papa's book."

"That's right, Miss Pandia, you finish it," Nanny said. "We could do with any money it makes."

"Yes, but that is not the main consideration," Pandia replied. "I cannot bear to think of anything that Papa wrote being wasted. He would be content if he helped even one person to understand the things that meant so much to him."

"Well, I'm going shopping!" Nanny said in her most practical tone. "Otherwise there'll be nothing to eat, and when you're working you'll be hungry, or at least you should be!"

Pandia had found it difficult to eat since she had returned home, not, as Nanny felt, because the food was not good enough for her, but because of the aching feeling in her breast.

It made it impossible for her to think of anything but a handsome face and twinkling eyes with strange vibrations of light that evoked a response within herself.

She went into her father's Study and sat down at his desk, forcing herself to think of him and not of the man who had said he wanted to help her with her translations.

Because of the way she was feeling, she found it harder to concentrate than ever she had in the past, and two hours later she thought despairingly that she had made very little headway.

She was finding it impossible to translate even the most simple words with the same sensitivity that her father had always shown.

"How can I be so stupid!" she asked herself.

She heard steps in the Hall and knew that Nanny had come back from the village.

She felt ashamed that she had wasted the morning when she should by this time have a substantial amount to show for the passing hours.

The door of the Study behind her opened but she did not turn her head and only said:

"Go away, Nanny! I do not deserve a good luncheon! I have simply not earned it!"

"I am sorry to hear that!" a voice replied.

But it was not Nanny who spoke.

For a moment Pandia thought she must be dreaming, then she jumped to her feet.

Standing in the doorway was Lord Silvester, and she thought that in the small room he seemed larger, more impressive, and more magnetic than he had ever been before.

For a moment she could only stare at him.

Then because there was a light in his eyes as if he was very pleased about something, she managed in a voice that did not sound like her own to ask:

"Why. . .are you. . .here?"

"I have found you!" he said. "Even though I was told that this was where you lived, I was desperately afraid I would be disappointed."

"B-but you. . .should not. . .find me!" Pandia gasped. "You should not. . .come here. . .unless. . .?"

She paused, and when he did not speak she went on:

"I. . .I cannot believe that. . .Selene. . ."

He walked towards her, and what she had been about to say died in her throat. She was only vividly conscious of him to the point where everything else flew out of her mind.

She could only look at him, her eyes filling her whole face, while her heart was thumping so loudly in her breast that she thought he must hear the sound of it.

Then she was not certain whether she moved or whether he put his arms round her.

All she knew was that she was close against him and he was kissing her wildly, passionately, demandingly, and the world stood still.

He kissed her until he carried her as he had before up to the peak of Olympus, and they were no longer human but one with the gods.

He kissed her until the fire on his lips was answered by a fire within herself, which rose from her breast into her throat so that when it touched his mouth she felt the wonder of it explode round them.

Then there was a conflagration within themselves and a blinding light that covered them and also came from their hearts.

Only when Pandia thought she could not feel such rapture and still be alive did Lord Silvester raise his head.

"How could you leave me?" he asked. "How could you have done anything so damnable as to deceive me in that ridiculous and absurd fashion?"

Before she could say anything, he was kissing her again, kissing her until she could only surrender herself to his mastery and know that she was no longer a separate human being but his and they were indivisible.

It might have been an hour or a century later that Pandia found herself sitting on the worn sofa in front of the fire with Lord Silvester's arms round her.

"You must. . .tell me how it is you are. . .here."

Her voice was very weak and she was conscious only of the closeness of him and that his magnetism made her thrill again and again like shafts of sunshine piercing her body.

"You have driven me nearly mad!" Lord Silvester replied. "When I left Linbourne House thinking you were with your husband, I thought everything I valued was lost to me."

Because Pandia had felt the same, she made an inarticulate little murmur and pressed her cheek against his shoulder.

"How could you do anything so crazy, so absurd, as to impersonate your sister?" he asked. "I suppose the average person would find it impossible to tell you apart, but. . ."

"H-how did you. . .know that was. . .what I did?" Pandia interrupted him.

His arms tightened round her before he said:

"You bewildered me, for I was quite certain when I kissed you that you had never been kissed before."

As if he must have it confirmed by her, he asked sharply, looking down at her:

"That is true?"

"Nobody. . .has kissed me. . .but you!"

He made a sound that was like a sigh of relief before he exclaimed:

"I knew it! I knew I would not be mistaken! At the same time, as I had no idea then that the Countess of Linbourne had a twin sister, it tortured me as no Christian Martyr has ever been tortured when I left you alone with your supposed husband, even though I knew something was very wrong."

"How. . .did you know that?"

He gave a little laugh.

"You know as well as I do that we can read each other's thoughts. When the Earl came into the room, though he apparently was unaware of it, I saw not only the expression in your eyes, but sensed also your consternation."

Then, as if he could not prevent himself from asking the question, Lord Silvester said:

"What happened that night?"

Pandia blushed and turned her face against his shoulder.

"N-nothing that you are. . .suspecting," she said a little incoherently.

He held her so tightly that it was almost impossible to breathe. Then he said:

"I suppose every man suffers the agony of Gethsemane at some time in his life, but I never want to experience that again! And I swear that if after we are married you make me as jealous as I was on Thursday night, I will murder you!"

"After we are. . .m-married?" Pandia faltered.

"We are being married after luncheon," Lord Silvester replied. "I have a Special Licence, and I saw your Church as I came into the village."

"What. . .what are you. . .saying?"

At the same time, she felt as if suddenly the Study were filled with the songs of angels and enveloped with a golden light that could only have come from a celestial sun.

Then as if she came back to reality she said in a very different voice:

"Y-you know. . .I. . .cannot marry you!"

"Why not?"

"Because. . .Selene has told. . .everybody that I am. . .dead!"

"I guessed that might have happened," Lord Silvester said, "but as far as I am concerned you are very much alive, my darling, and I have every intention of marrying you."

"But. . .you must not. . ." Pandia began.

She stopped, then said:

"First you must finish your story. . .how did you. . . find out about me? I. . .I must know."

"As I had already arranged," Lord Silvester began, and she knew he spoke with an effort, "I spent Friday morning seeing my Publisher and signing my books for reviewers."

He paused before he continued:

"Then I remembered somewhat belatedly that I had promised to dine with the Foreign Secretary. I had been to see him immediately on my arrival in England, and he invited me particularly to dine with him on Friday evening."

Pandia stiffened.

"And Selene was there!"

"Exactly!" he agreed. "And as soon as I saw her I knew she was not you!"

"How. . .could you know that? We look. . .exactly alike."

"Not as far as I am concerned."

Pandia looked at him, and he said:

"The expression in your sister's eyes would have told

me she was not you, even if I had not been aware when we shook hands that something was missing."

"My. . .vibrations!"

"Of course," Lord Silvester agreed. "I had felt them when you were beside me in the Church."

"So. . .did I."

"When I touched your sister's hand and looked into her eyes, I knew unmistakably that she must have a twin sister!"

"It was clever of you. . .but. . .you did not. . .say so to her?"

"No, of course not," he answered. "I merely made a few remarks on some of the subjects that you and I had discussed at the Castle, and when it was obvious that she had not the slightest idea of what I was talking about, I was convinced that I knew the secret you had been hiding from me."

"Then what. . .did you do?"

"After that everything was very easy!"

"How could it have. . .been?"

"First thing the next morning," he replied, "I went to see your father's Publisher, only to find that he did not work on Saturdays! I therefore had to follow him to his weekend retreat, which is outside London."

He smiled as he said:

"But before that I obtained a Special Licence from the Archbishop of Canterbury, who also happened to be dining with the Foreign Secretary on Friday evening, to marry somebody called 'Pandia Hunyadi.' "

"You were quite certain I. . .existed?"

"Absolutely, and especially after I looked in your father's last book and found his dedication: 'To my daughter, Pandia,' " he answered. "Your father's Publisher confirmed what I knew already, and gave me what I did not know, your address."

"How could. . .you have been so. . .clever?"

"It was not as difficult or as nerve-racking as finding a manuscript that had been hidden for several thousands of years and then translating it."

He kissed Pandia before she could reply, and when he could speak again, he said:

"Now I can help you to finish your father's book, and I have already told his Publishers that I will write a Foreword to it, and I expect it to be given the same treatment that my Publishers give to my books."

"Will you. . .really do that?" Pandia cried. "How can you be so wonderful. . .so kind? I do want Papa's book to be a success!"

"It will be," Lord Silvester said. "We will make sure of that! In the meantime, you have to help me with my book, and that means we are leaving for Morocco at the end of the week."

"Do you mean. . .that I am. . .coming with you?"

"I am certainly not leaving my wife behind!"

"And. . .we are being. . .married. . .as you say. . .this afternoon?"

Even as Pandia said the words she felt they could not be true and she was merely dreaming what she thought he had said.

"We are going to be married," Lord Silvester said firmly, "and I think you might be hospitable enough to ask me to stay in this very attractive house!"

"Stay. , .here?"

"Why not?" he asked. "I have a house of my own, which I am going to tell you about, but there is not time to go there at the moment because we will have a lot of things to buy in London before we leave."

Pandia gave a little cry.

"You are going too. . .quickly! You must be aware that I cannot. . .go to London. . .and I cannot. . .marry you because of Selene."

Lord Silvester put his free hand under her chin and turned her face up to his.

"Now listen to me, my darling," he said. "I am not a fool, and seeing how you are living here, and having learnt from your father's Publishers how poor you have been, I know quite well what your sister did."

He paused before he went on:

"I had a long talk with the Earl at the dinner-party and he told me how your sister, alone and orphaned after her father and mother died, was brought up by your grandparents."

His voice was sarcastic before he finished:

"They could not leave her to starve, even though they had been horrified at the way in which your mother had run away with an Hungarian Tutor."

Because Pandia felt embarrassed by what he was saying, she tried to move her face from his fingers, but he would not let her go, and said:

"If your sister could pronounce you dead, she can also think up a story to explain how, after all, you are alive."

"How can she. . .do such a. . .thing?" Pandia asked in a frightened tone.

"If she cannot invent an explanation, I can. You could have been left for dead in the desert, captured by Bedouins from whom I was able to rescue you, or alternatively, like Romulus and Remus, you might have been nursed by a wolf!"

His eyes were twinkling and he was laughing as he spoke, but because it sounded so embarrassing, Pandia blushed.

As if he understood, he set her free.

She hid her face against him and he said:

"But as I will not have you upset, we will have our honeymoon first and go to Morocco. When we get back, if it pleases you, you shall dazzle the Social World as your sister has done."

"I. . .I do not want. . .that," Pandia said quickly, "I just want to. . .be with you!"

"That is what I want too," he said. "So when we do return to England we will go to the house I have just been left, but did not expect, in my Godfather's Will."

"He left you a house?"

"A house and Estate in Devonshire," Lord Silvester replied, "which I visited a long time ago. It is very beautiful and close to the sea. I think we will find it the

perfect place to finish your father's book and mine
before we set out once again on our adventures."

"Is that what we are going to do?"

"That is what I hope you will want to do."

"Of course I want it!" Pandia cried. "I want it more
than I can ever tell you. . .but I am afraid. . .terribly
afraid. . .that it is something I. . .should not do."

"You have no decisions to make," he said. "You will
marry me, and I have no intention of hiding my wife
away and letting nobody see her!"

His lips twisted a little cynically as he went on:

"We will save your sister's face, and doubtless her
marriage, by making our story very plausible, and, my
darling, I shall be very proud of being married to the
most beautiful goddess who ever came down from
Olympus!"

He drew her a little closer as he added:

"We will live the life of the gods, which is, as we
both know, the perfection that all men seek, but few
are fortunate enough to find."

As if he wanted to make sure for himself that she was
real and he was not dreaming, he kissed her possessively,
passionately, and in a way that was different from the
way he had kissed her before.

Then when they both were breathless he said:

"God, how I love you! And I do not intend to wait
any longer to make you my wife!"

He rose to his feet as he spoke, and said:

"I will go to make arrangements with the Vicar for us
to be married before two-thirty, which I believe is the
prescribed time in a Protestant Church."

Because of the way he spoke, Pandia could not help
asking:

"Would you. . .rather we were. . .married in any other
sort?"

"It does not matter to me what the Church is called,"
he replied, "so long as it makes you legally my wife.
What really matters is that we are together, as we have
been in the past, and this time for eternity."

There was a solemn note in his voice which made Pandia know that he was speaking from his heart.

Because she could not help herself, she put out her arms to draw his head down to hers.

"I love you!" she said. "I. . .love you so much that. . .it is going to take. . .all this life. . .at any rate. . .to tell you how much!"

He held her against him so that their bodies seemed to melt into each other's. Then he said:

"Go and find something appropriate in which to be married, my lovely one. Whatever you wear, you will look to me like Persephone after you forced me to go down into Hades to find you."

Pandia laughed as he opened the Study door and went into the Hall.

He put on his fur-lined coat which he had laid on a chair and picked up his hat, then once again he put his fingers under her chin to turn her face up to his.

"Promise me you will not vanish before I come back," he said. "I feel I have performed all the twelve labours of Hercules in my efforts to find you, and I could not bear another dozen waiting for me if you disappear!"

"I. . .I will be. . .here," Pandia replied, "and do not let. . .anything happen to you. . .between here and the Vicarage!"

She thought as she spoke that it would make him laugh, and it did.

At the same time, she told herself that although he had been to Mecca and had risked his life many times, she was still afraid of losing him because it seemed impossible that she could be so happy and that her life could be so changed as if by the waving of a magic wand.

Only when the front door had closed behind him did she run to the kitchen to find out if Nanny was there.

"Nanny, Nanny! I am to be married this afternoon! And I am so happy that I cannot believe it is true!"

Nanny stared at her. Then she burst into tears.

"It's what I've prayed for, Miss Pandia," she said. "I

thought you'd never find a decent man living in this place with nobody to see you, and Miss Selene pretending you don't even exist!"

"I not only exist, but I am the happiest person in the whole world!"

Because her face was so radiant and she looked so lovely, tears poured down Nanny's face.

* * *

Nanny was the only witness at their wedding, and she watched Lord Silvester take Pandia up the aisle on his arm.

The Vicar was waiting for them at the Chancel steps and the organ was playing very softly.

To Pandia the angels were singing and the whole Church seemed vibrant with love.

There was a gown amongst Selene's things which she was certain her sister had bought for a garden-party or some other very important occasion.

Of white chiffon trimmed with real lace, it was so beautiful and at the same time so spectacular that she could understand that, having worn it once, Selene would think it impossible ever to wear it again.

It was the loveliest gown Pandia had ever imagined she could own.

There was a huge picture-hat to wear with it, but she found a wreath of white flowers that went with one of the evening-gowns and Nanny made her a veil of white tulle.

She had nothing to carry in her hands and was therefore very touched when Silvester brought from the carriage in which he had travelled from London a box in which she found a bouquet of white orchids.

"How could you have been so sure you would. . .marry me today?" she asked.

"I did not believe there could be any good reason why, once I found you, you should refuse to marry me!"

He thought there was still a question in her eyes and added:

"You see, I knew, my darling, that you loved me just as I love you!"

"How were you. . .certain of. . .that?"

"When I kissed you at the Castle you gave me your soul, and that was what I had always been wanting and had never received from any other woman."

He saw the expression in her eyes and added:

"You have no reason to be jealous, my precious. Of course there have been women in my life, some of them of very strange nationalities, but I have always, and this is the truth, been looking for the woman I knew was the other half of myself."

He smiled before he went on:

"My studies in all the strange languages and manuscripts I have found told me that this is what, all through the ages, other men sought, usually to be disappointed."

He kissed her lightly before he said:

"When I sat down next to you in the Church I knew I had found the woman I had been seeking."

"But. . .suppose I had really been married. . .like Selene?"

"Then, like Paris and Helen of Troy, I would have snatched you away and started a war or a scandal."

"I am glad you did. . .not have to do. . .that. . .but I am still. . .afraid that I should not really. . .marry you."

"You have no choice in the matter," he answered.

When they went back to the house from the Church he produced a bottle of champagne and insisted that Nanny should drink their health.

"You've made me very happy, M'Lord," Nanny said. "I was worried about my baby living here on her own. Yet somehow I thought one day God'd answer my prayers and she'd find the husband she deserved."

"I doubt if I will ever be that," Silvester said, "but we will be very happy, Nanny! And just as my wife will now start a very different life from what she has lived before, so will you!"

Nanny looked surprised, and he continued:

"We are going to Morocco for our honeymoon. I therefore want you to close up this house and take everything that Her Ladyship wants, and of course yourself, to our new home in Devonshire."

"Do you. . .really mean that. . .M'Lord?" Nanny asked in a trembling voice.

"Certainly I mean it!" Silvester replied. "And you must be aware that nobody but you could get the Nurseries ready!"

Nanny's eyes shone through her tears, and Pandia made an inarticulate little murmur and hid her blushes against her husband's shoulder.

Only when Nanny had gone back to the kitchen with the tears still running down her cheeks did Pandia say shyly:

"How could you say. . .that to Nanny? And how can you be. . .sure?"

"Of course I am sure," Silvester replied, "and that is why, my precious one, we must have our home ready for our family, and somebody we can trust to take care of our babies when we set out for new horizons and new inspiration for the books we will write together."

"That is what Papa would. . .want me to do, but I still cannot. . .believe it is. . .true that I shall see all. . .the places I thought I would know only in my imagination."

"You will see them, live in them, and find life at times very uncomfortable," he said. "At the same time, my darling, we shall be together."

"That is all I want," Pandia replied. "Oh, darling, darling Silvester, how can it be true that I have. . .found you and that you. . .love me and everything is so. . .perfect?"

"I think you did not have enough faith in fate, and your instinct should have told you that there is always something we do not expect round the next corner."

He laughed before he added:

"In our ignorance we call it 'destiny,' but it is really

the Wheel of Life and Rebirth, and the irresistible magic of love."

"You are saying all the things I want to hear and which I want to understand," Pandia cried.

"I will teach you about them, amongst other things."

Then as he kissed her again he said:

"Now I am going to take you upstairs and we are going to rest after what has been a very exciting, emotional experience, the first and last time either of us will be married."

Pandia blushed, and as with his arms round her Silvester walked with her up the small staircase, she whispered:

"It seems. . .rather. . .shocking to go to bed in the daytime!"

He laughed and his laughter rang out in the small house.

"Now, my darling, you are being very English and very prosaic," he said, "but I think your father would have told you that for the Hungarians, together with a great number of other peoples, love-making is not confined to certain hours, days, or weeks."

He pulled her closer to him and went on:

"Love is something which should be available when we want it, and I want you now, at this very moment, and I feel as if I have already waited a thousand centuries!"

As he spoke, Pandia opened the door of her mother's bedroom.

It was a pretty and attractive room, and as she had dressed in it the fire had been lit, and she thought it was just as lovely as the bedroom at the Castle in which Silvester had first kissed her.

Then it was impossible to think of anything but that they were together!

He lifted first the wreath from her head, then the veil, and took the pins from her hair so that it fell in great waves over her shoulders.

Then he pulled her against his heart and she felt him undoing her gown.

"You make me shy," she murmured.

"I adore you when you are shy."

Her gown slipped to the ground and she hid her face against his shoulder, whispering:

"Please. . .do not. . .look at. . .me!"

"I want to look at you, touch you, and kiss you from the top of your head to the soles of your feet."

The passion in his voice made it impossible for her to breathe.

Then as he carried her to the bed, she felt the light that came from him vibrate through her until she quivered with a wild and uncontrollable ecstasy.

*   *   *

A long time later, when it was dark outside and there was only the golden firelight, Pandia asked in a whisper:

"Do you. . .still love me?"

"That is the question I should be asking you, my precious one," he said. "There is no need for me to tell you that I not only adore you and worship you, but I did not believe it possible for any man to be as happy as I am at this moment!"

"I have. . .really made you. . .happy?"

"So happy, my darling, that I am afraid that what the gods have given me the gods might take away, and you will fly back to Olympus."

"I will never do that," Pandia said, "because now I am with you, and although I cannot. . .express it as beautifully as you do. . .I know that I am not. . .a goddess, but a. . .woman, and yet I am living in a. . .special Heaven to which you have. . .carried me."

"Now I want to ask you that question," Silvester said. "I have made you happy?"

" 'Happy' is not the right word," Pandia replied. "You have picked the stars from the sky and put them in my breast. I have kissed the moon. . .and felt the heat of the sun. I have dived into the depths of the. . .ocean and found. . .you at the very. . .bottom of it."

She spoke in a rapt little voice which he did not miss. Then she added so softly that he could hardly hear:

"I had no. . .idea that. . .making love could be so. . .glorious. . .so wonderful. . .and now I know why the gods came down to earth. . .to make love. . .like human beings."

"That is what I wanted you to feel, my darling one," Silvester said, "and I have only just begun to teach you about love."

His lips moved across her forehead as he spoke. Then he gave a little laugh.

"How could you really think you could pretend to be a married woman when you were so pure, untouched, and completely innocent?"

"I did not think. . .anybody would be aware of that. . .unless like you they had. . .dared to. . .kiss me."

Even as she spoke she remembered that the Earl had wanted not only to kiss her but also to make love to her, and she gave a little shiver.

As if he knew what she was thinking, Silvester said:

"Exactly! That is why, my darling, you will never try to deceive me or anybody else again. And never, never play the part that your sister asked of you! I consider it was an outrageous thing for her to ask you to do!"

"She. . .she only asked me to. . .go to a Funeral!"

"Where I was waiting for you!"

"I could not have. . .guessed you would have done anything as. . .shocking as. . .coming to my bedroom!"

He turned round so that he could look down at her where she lay against the pillows.

Her hair was streaming over her shoulders as it had the night he had come to her room at the Castle, and her eyes, shining in the light of the fire, looked up at him.

"I knew in that moment," he said, "that however long it took, whatever the difficulties, you would be mine."

"Did you. . .really feel like that? I thought when I. . .sent you away that I had. . .lost you forever!"

"If one wants something enough," Silvester said, "even the gods cannot prevent us from having it. I wanted you and I was prepared to sacrifice the whole world to gain you!"

"Oh, darling, I am so glad!" Pandia cried. "But. . .just supposing. . .believing me to be married. . .you had gone off to Morocco and. . .forgotten me?"

"I would never have forgotten you," he said, "and like the gods, I was prepared to fight in every way I knew to get you, even if it meant carrying you away by force!"

Pandia laughed.

Then she realised that the way he had spoken with a determination that was so much a part of him had brought again the fire to his eyes, and she was aware that his heart was beating against hers.

She could feel the flames flickering again within herself, moving up from her breast to her lips.

It was the fire that raced in her blood and which Selene had been right in saying was something their father had given them.

It was a fire which was not only very human but also Divine.

Her husband's lips came down on hers as she felt her whole body surrender itself to him, the flames leaping higher and higher.

"You are mine," he cried passionately. "Mine, and I worship you."

"Love me. . .Oh! Silvester. . .love me," Pandia whispered.

Then once again he carried her as if in a chariot towards the stars, and as he made her his she knew that their love was glorious, magnetic, irresistible, and no power on earth could withstand it.

ABOUT THE AUTHOR

Barbara Cartland, the world's most famous romantic novelist, who is also an historian, playwright, lecturer, political speaker and television personality, has now written over 350 books and sold over 350 million books throughout the world.

She has also had many historical works published and has written four autobiographies as well as the biographies of her mother and that of her brother, Ronald Cartland, who was the first Member of Parliament to be killed in World War II. This book has a preface by Sir Winston Churchill and has just been republished with an introduction by Sir Arthur Bryant.

Love at the Helm, a novel written with the help and inspiration of the late Earl Mountbatten of Burma, Uncle of His Royal Highness Prince Philip, is being sold for the Mountbatten Memorial Trust.

In 1978, Miss Cartland sang an Album of Love Songs with the Royal Philharmonic Orchestra.

In 1976, by writing twenty-one books, she broke the world record and has continued for the following six years with 24, 20, 23, 24, six, and 25. She is in the *Guinness Book of World Records* as currently the top-selling authoress in the world.

She is unique in that she was #1 and #2 in the Dalton List of BestSellers, and one week had four books in the top twenty.

In private life Barbara Cartland, who is a Dame of the Order of St. John of Jerusalem, Chairman of the St. John Council in Hertfordshire and Deputy President of the St. John Ambulance Brigade, has also fought for better conditions and salaries for midwives and nurses.

Barbara Cartland is deeply interested in vitamin therapy and is President of the British National Association for Health. Her book, *The Magic of Honey*, has sold throughout the world and is translated into many languages.

Her designs, *Decorating with Love*, are being sold all over the USA and the National Home Fashions League made her "Woman of Achievement" in 1981.

Barbara Cartland Romances (book of cartoons) has just been published in Great Britain and the United States, and several countries in Europe carry the strip cartoons of her novels.